Beware the Claw!

Beware the Claw!

by R. A. Noonan

ALADDIN PAPERBACKS

First Aladdin Paperbacks edition March 1996

Aladdin Paperbacks
An imprint of Simon & Schuster
Children's Publishing Division
1230 Avenue of the Americas
New York, NY 10020

Printed and bound in the United States of America

10 9 8 7 6 5 4 3 2 1

Library of Congress Cataloging-in-Publication Data

Noonan, R. A.
Beware the claw! / by R. A. Noonan. — 1st Aladdin
Paperbacks ed.
p. cm. — (Monsterville ; #5)
Summary: While eleven-year-old Darcy and her cousins try to find a way to get a yeti back home to Monsterville, she also worries that her "sister" wants to return to her life as a fairy.
ISBN 0-689-71867-5
[1. Yeti—Fiction. 2. Fairies—Fiction.] I. Title. II. Series: Noonan, R. A. Monsterville ; #5.
PZ7.N753Be 1996
[Fic]—dc20 95-31187

Beware the Claw!

Prologue

The giant beast tore through the brambles.

"Gr-r-r-r!" it bellowed, clawing away dead leaves. Its wide, fur-covered legs moved forward with huge steps.

It had been traveling long and far. It was in no mood for delays.

"Woe to the creature that blocks my path!" it snarled, holding its twisted paw to the sky. Its claws were sharp, like a deadly set of knives.

White snowflakes fell from the sky, but the creature didn't care. It liked the snow. It liked the cold.

Better to freeze the humans who trespass in these woods. The creature let out a roar as it lumbered ahead. Nothing could stop it now.

Beware the bite of the beastly bear.

Beware the Claw!

Pop! A cinder burst in the fireplace, making Fiona Mackie jump. "What was that?"

"Just the fire." Eleven-year-old Darcy Ryan pulled her younger cousin closer on the sofa. With the lights out and shadows dancing across the room, no wonder Fiona was spooked. She was only six.

"I thought it was the Claw," Fiona whispered, burrowing her head into the crook of Darcy's arm.

"It could be," Sam Mackie said. "The Claw loves to come out at night in snowstorms. And it's snowing like crazy out there."

Outside the wide, paned window of the Ryans' living room, white flakes drifted through the night. Since it was Friday, their parents had agreed to let Fiona and Sam stay over at the Ryan ranch. It was the perfect night to huddle by a warm fire and play games. But somehow they'd gotten on the

3

subject of the Claw, Montana's most notorious woodland creature.

"D-d-does the Claw ever break into houses?" Fiona asked, her voice quavering.

"He's unstoppable," Sam said, his dark eyes glimmering. Thirteen-year-old Sam was usually pretty serious about things. But sometimes he liked to make his pesky little sister squirm.

"Cut it out, Sam," Francie said. "You're scaring Fee." She stood up and tossed her ginger hair over the shoulder of her cable-knit sweater. "I'm going to make cocoa. Why don't you guys break out Monopoly or Nintendo or something?"

"I want to know more about the Claw," Fiona insisted as Francie disappeared into the kitchen. "What does it look like? Has it ever hurt anyone? Does it ever . . . *eat children*?"

"It's just an old legend," Darcy said. "Some hunter probably saw a bear in the woods and made up a big story about it."

"The Claw is no ordinary bear," Sam insisted. "Hunters say it's an awesome ugly sight. And its right paw is contorted."

"*Cavorted*? What's that mean?" Fiona asked. Her dark eyes were bright with fear.

"Contorted. It's sort of . . . twisted," Sam said in an eerie voice. Shadows made his eyes look like two black holes. "The paw is huge, with

4

talons that are six inches long. Six inches!"

"Oooh!" Fiona hugged Darcy tight.

Darcy patted her cousin's shoulder and tried to imagine it. Six-inch nails weren't very practical in the woods. And she'd lived her whole life in this wooded section of the Bitterroot Mountains. Darcy had always thought the Claw legend was sort of silly, but Sam made it sound real. His rasping voice sent a little chill up her spine.

"That giant paw is how the beast got its name," Sam continued. "That, and the fact that it growls at everyone it meets. It clenches its deadly teeth and snarls, *'Beware the Claw! Beware the Claw!'*"

Shadows danced over the silent room. *It's only a story*, Darcy reminded herself. She was getting goose bumps!

A sudden rumble thundered.

"What's that?" Fiona said, tensing.

Darcy glanced over at the fireplace, where a log had rolled to the back of the grate. "It's just the fire, Fee. Calm down."

"I can't help it." Fiona screwed her face up in agony. "The Claw stuff is scary, but I want to hear all about it."

She turned to the wide window. "Do you think it's really out there? Tromping through the snow?"

"No one has spotted the Claw for years," Sam said quietly. "But sometimes, if you're very still,

5

you can hear him outside your window."

"Really?" Fiona's face was pale as she stared at the window.

"You'll hear him scratching," Sam whispered. "Scraping . . . trying to get in."

Fiona's mouth dropped open in horror.

"What's wrong?" Darcy asked.

"It's—it's—" Gaping, Fiona pointed across the room.

"Listen," Sam hissed.

Kreeee! Kreeee! It was a scraping sound.

Darcy swung her head around and blinked. Long silver prongs were scraping at the window!

Fiona covered her eyes as Sam and Darcy crept toward the window for a better look. Each scrape of the silver talons made Darcy's heart thump in her chest.

A yard from the window, Sam held Darcy back and let out a yelp. "Run for your life! It's the Claw!"

"Whaaaah!" Fiona shrieked. She bolted from the sofa, dashing toward the hall.

Darcy froze in place. The silver prongs were still scraping the window, but there was something else. . . .

Pink mittens attached to the long nails. Did the Claw wear pink mittens?

I don't think so, Darcy thought, stepping closer to the window.

The mittens belonged to a girl in a green down jacket—with a very familiar face.

"Francie!" Darcy tapped on the window, and Francie stepped forward, peering back at her. "What's that in your hand?" Darcy shouted through the glass.

With a sheepish grin, Francie held the kitchen utensil in plain view.

"A pasta fork?" Darcy rolled her eyes. "Very funny, guys."

"Yes!" Sam said, raising his arms in a victory sign. "Way to scare 'em! Even Darcy went for it."

"Sort of," Darcy admitted.

"So it was just a trick?" Fiona asked, hanging back in the hallway.

"Just a joke," Sam said, waving Francie in. "A really *good* joke."

Ten minutes later, the foursome was sitting by the fire sipping hot cocoa. Francie's wet jacket was hanging in the mudroom, and she was perched on the hearth in her robe and fluffy slippers.

On the coffee table, Fiona was building a tower of marshmallows.

Sam swiped one from the top of the stack and dropped it into his mug. "They're meant for eating," he said.

"Hey! Don't wreck it!" Fiona snapped.

"Don't push it, Sam. After that joke, you're skating on thin ice," Darcy reminded him.

"It was all in good fun," Francie said, nudging Darcy with one slipper.

"I know," Darcy said, smiling at Francie. The two girls were almost like sisters. Everyone in Whiterock thought that Francie was just staying with Darcy and her mom so that she could finish school here.

Only Darcy, Sam, Fiona, and Darcy's best friend Brook knew the truth. Francie needed a home because she'd recently turned into a girl. Before that, she'd been a fairy—a magical, winged creature you could hold in the palm of your hand.

But Francie's story was just one amazing part of the kids' adventures. The real wonder was the town they'd discovered on the other side of the Bitterroots.

A town of monsters.

Monsterville . . . Darcy loved to visit there. And who would've guessed that she'd find a sister in a town of monsters . . . or that she'd be living right here in her home.

"Ooooch!" Darcy giggled as Francie nudged her again. "Your slippers are tickling me."

"No wonder," Sam said, eyeing the slippers. They were huge, furry replicas of bear paws. "Where'd you get those things?"

"From a catalog." Francie smoothed back the fake fur and pointed to the plastic toes. "Aren't they great? They even have tiny bear toes molded on the bottom."

"You've got strange taste," Sam said.

"You're just jealous," Francie insisted.

Fiona knocked over the marshmallow tower, then started building a house. "I hope it snows all night."

"Me, too," Francie agreed. "I want to go skiing. And snowshoeing. And sledding."

"Just watch out for the Claw," Fiona warned. "He might pop out of a snowdrift and attack you."

"It's just a legend," Darcy reminded her. She nudged Sam. "See what you did?"

"I was just repeating the stuff I heard at school," Sam said. "Can I help it if I'm a fantastic storyteller?"

🦇 🦇 🦇

"I'll race you to the bottom!" Fiona called back to Darcy as she coasted down a snowy incline.

"You're on." Darcy pointed her skis downhill.

It was midmorning, and snow was still falling. As soon as they'd finished breakfast, the kids had decided to bundle up and go cross-country skiing on the local trails.

Sam and Francie were lagging behind, taking their good old time, but Darcy didn't care. She was happy to be outside, gliding over fresh powder. Saturday always held a certain magic for Darcy. And today was even more fun since everything had been frosted with white icing.

Wind stung her cheeks as Darcy soared down the hill. Ahead, Fiona was waiting in a narrow clearing surrounded by snow-laden trees.

"I won! I won!" Fiona crowed, jumping up and down on her skis.

"You did," Darcy said, sliding to a halt. "But I bet I can make a bigger snow angel than you."

"No way!" Fiona took off her skis and hurried over to a snowdrift. "I'm going to make a big, fat angel. Then I'll decorate her with eyes made of pine cones."

"Good luck finding anything under all this snow," Darcy said. She fell back into a mound of snow and fanned her arms and legs through the white powder, then stood up.

A perfect angel. Now she just needed to give her a face.

Kneeling beside the angel, she scooped up a handful of snow. "I'll give her wide eyes, and a friendly smile," she said.

Bink! Pop!

What was that?

"Fiona?" Darcy called. The sounds were coming from the woods, where Fiona was rooting for pine cones.

"D-D-Darcy!" Snow crunched as Fiona waddled out from under a snow-covered tree. Her chin was quivering. "There's something . . . someone in the woods!"

"Probably just an animal," Darcy said reassuringly.

Ping! Punk! The noises echoed from the woods.

"It's *not*!" Fiona insisted. "It's something weird."

She clutched Darcy's arm. "Maybe it's the Claw!"

"Fee . . ." Darcy shook her head. "Bears don't make noise like that. It sounds like . . . like the Fourth of July."

Curious, Darcy headed toward the edge of the woods. Fiona followed, careful to stay behind her older cousin.

The tall evergreens were blanketed by thick snow, forming a canopy overhead. The forest was dark and frozen, a hidden world of sugarcoated brambles and dwarf trees.

Darcy peered into the darkness and blinked.

Pop! Plink!

With each noise, a colored light flashed before her eyes.

Boink! Plunk! Bing! A purple light winked. A blue light flashed.

What was going on?

Suddenly an orange light exploded near Darcy's eyes, sending her reeling backward. . . .

Her feet slipped out from under her, and Darcy toppled back onto a snowdrift.

"What was it?" Fiona asked, kneeling beside her. "Was it the Claw?"

"No." Darcy shook her head in confusion. "It's not a bear, either." She stood up and brushed the snow off her pants. "But this weird light flashed right in front of—"

Ping! Boink!

Just then a purple star exploded near the edge of the woods. The girls stared at the burst of light. As soon as the light died out, a tiny figure materialized. It hovered in the air, its papery wings holding up the pint-size body.

Fiona's eyes widened. "It's a fairy!"

"A whole squadron of them," Darcy added. There were flashing lights everywhere!

"Hoshi's the name," the purple sprite chirped.

"You must be pretty bright, little girl. Most kids aren't wise to us."

"I've met fairies before," Fiona said.

"Is that right?" Hoshi nodded, then turned to Darcy. "Sorry if Neona knocked you over, kid. She's outta control right now."

As the fairy spoke, the flashing orange light soared out of the woods and looped around her.

"Outta control!" the orange fairy snapped. "Can I help it if my compass is frozen? And who can fly right in this heavy snow!"

"Now girls! Don't fight," called a third voice. A blue light flashed under a pine tree. The fairy landed on a frozen limb and let out a sneeze.

"Bless you," Darcy offered.

"Thank you, dear," the blue fairy said. "I just can't take this cold."

"If you guys hate cold so much, what are you doing out here?" Darcy asked.

"We're on our way to a fairy convention," said Hoshi. "But it's hard to fly straight in a snowstorm."

"We lost our bearings, and now we're missing all the fun," Neona griped with a flash of orange.

"Aaaa-*choo*!" The blue fairy belted out a second sneeze. This one sent her sputtering into a pile of snow.

"Oh, Beryl!" Hoshi lamented, fluttering to her friend's aid. "You're in bad shape, kiddo."

14

Just then laughter sailed down the hill, followed by Sam and Francie.

"What's the holdup down there?" Sam said. He hadn't seen the fairies yet.

But Francie saw them right away. "Hi ya, girls!" she gasped. "It's me! Your old buddy." She pulled off her pink wool cap and her ginger hair spilled down her back.

"Francie?" Hoshi blinked.

"Pinch me, I'm dreamin'," Neona said. Hoshi gave her toe a squeeze, and Neona let out a yelp. "It's just a figure of speech," she grumbled.

Sam ducked as Neona zipped past his ear. "More fairies? I can't believe it."

"Well *I* can't believe what I'm seeing, either," Hoshi exclaimed. "Our fairy friend has grown— about a zillion inches!"

"I didn't just get bigger," Francie said with a laugh. "I turned into a girl. And believe me, it took some potent witches' spells to keep me that way."

"Totally weird," Neona said.

"Totally cool," Hoshi sputtered.

"Totally, t-t-aaaa-*choo*!" Beryl sneezed.

"Gezoomheit," Fiona said.

"Oh, you poor thing," Darcy said as Beryl landed on her shoulder. "You need to get out of the snow."

"It's murder on my compass," Beryl agreed.

"Besides, I think my fairy dust is trying to freeze over. We should've landed in Monsterville hours ago."

"Monsterville?" Francie gasped. "Don't tell me the convention is there this year."

"It's there," Hoshi said. "You ever heard of the place?"

"We've . . . *heard* of it," Sam said cautiously.

"Are you kidding?" Francie smiled. "Monsterville was my ticket to freedom. That's where I turned into a girl."

"No kidding," Hoshi said with a flash of purple.

"I hope it's not contagious," Neona said worriedly.

"Me, too," Sam added with a wry look.

Francie held one mitten over her eyes to see through the blinding snow. "You're not too far from the entrance," she said.

"And we know the way," Darcy said as hope curled inside her. She could never resist a visit to Monsterville. "If you want, we can take you there."

Blue, purple, and orange lights blinked in unison.

"Gr-r-reat idea!" Hoshi chirped. "We've been flying in circles so long, I'm getting dizzy."

"Just point the way," Neona said.

Normally the fairies could have sped ahead of the kids, but in the snowstorm skis seemed to be the fastest way to go.

If only Brook could come with us, Darcy thought as she pressed forward through the lilting white flakes. Shy Brook Lauer, one of Darcy's best friends, had recently discovered Monsterville and was dying to go back. But Brook was away for the weekend, skiing at a resort. Too bad!

Fiona offered Beryl a ride in her pocket, and the blue fairy gratefully tucked herself in. Hoshi hitched a ride in the hood of Francie's jacket, and Neona rode on Sam's shoulder, griping all the way.

"You can cut the cheerful act, Francie-pantsie," Neona said as Francie brushed snowflakes from Fiona's hat. "Nobody can be that happy as a girl."

"You always did have a glum way of putting things," Francie teased, smiling at Neona. "I *love* being a girl."

"And I'm glad Francie's our cousin now," Fiona chimed in. "Sammy likes her, too. Don't ya, Sam?"

"Sure, squirt," Sam said quietly.

"But what about the kids out there who need pixie favors?" Hoshi added. "It must feel awful to let them down."

"I—well—," Francie stammered. "I never really thought about that." She turned away and concentrated on sliding up a narrow hill.

"Don't you miss helping people out?" Hoshi prodded.

Taken by surprise, Francie turned back. "Well,

sure. I mean, I've always enjoyed helping people."

"Such a shame." Neona clucked. "All those powers wasted away."

"Aren't there times when you wish you still had your pixie dust?" Hoshi asked.

"Well, sure," Francie said again. "Especially when it's time to clean my room."

Wind stung Darcy's cheeks as she listened to the conversation. It sounded like Francie really missed being a fairy!

Just then Fiona tugged on Darcy's sleeve. Her face was pale, her dark eyes concerned. "Did you hear that?" she whispered. "Francie wants her fairy dust back!"

"Shh!" Darcy pointed to the blue fairy dozing in Fiona's pocket. "You'll wake Beryl."

"But I'm worried," Fiona said so that only Darcy could hear her. "What if Francie changes her mind? What if she decides to become a fairy again?"

Darcy shuddered. She didn't want to think about it.

She glanced back at Francie and the two pixies. "You crack me up!" Francie exclaimed, doubling over. Neona and Hoshi were laughing over a fairy joke. The three of them were really hitting it off.

Darcy bit her lower lip. She'd finally gotten the sister she'd always wanted. Was she going to lose her?

Darcy couldn't stop worrying during the trip up the hill and into the cave. Even the relief of getting out of the snowstorm seemed trivial compared to the thought of losing Francie.

Once they passed through the golden arched door—a special door that only certain people could see—her thoughts turned to the magical land of monsters.

As the kids trekked through the crystal tunnel, Darcy noticed the way the fairies brought the place to life. Their lights made glimmering shows on the walls. An orange sparkler. Purple stars. Blue bursts of light. No wonder Francie like being around them.

"Leave it to the monsters to move to a place so hidden even *we* couldn't find it," Neona pointed out.

"You can't blame them," Sam said.

"They came here to get away from all the bad things in the world," Fiona said.

"Like wars and pollution and homework," said Darcy.

"And brussels sprouts," added Fiona.

The tinkling sound of icicles greeted them at the end of the cave . . .

Along with two imposing figures.

"Good afternoon, Samuel . . . Frances," came the raspy voice of the cloaked figure. It was the Grim Reaper, the mayor of Monsterville. Beside him, Draku cowered under his red silk cape.

"G. R.! Look who we brought," Fiona said, tugging on his cloak. "Fairies!"

Darcy held back a shiver. She never understood how Fiona could cozy up to Mr. Death. Maybe Fee just didn't grasp the guy's mission in the world.

"Ah! At last!" G. R.'s bony hands clapped around his staff. "We were just about to send a search party out for you. Your friends are quite worried."

Draku lowered his cape, giving them all a glimpse of his vampire fangs. "Just what we need. More dust-toting fireflies."

Neona darted over to the vampire and flashed orange before his eyes. "Feeling grumpy, lumpy?"

He scowled. "These fairies are out of control!"

"Now, Draku . . . ," G. R. soothed.

"They've sprinkled pixie dust over Main Street.

The werewolves can't stop sneezing," Draku lamented. "They covered Ahmose's pyramid with chocolate frosting. And my crypt! They actually wanted to dust the place out. Can you imagine?"

"Sounds like the party's already begun," Hoshi said.

"Let's do it!" Neona tossed an orange cloud at Draku. The glittering dust fell into his jet-black hair.

"Oooh!" A wide smile suddenly spread across his face. "I *guess* the fairy convention isn't so bad. In fact, I'm kind of beginning to like it."

"Neona!" Francie tried to hide a laugh. "You are terrible!"

"Just a touch of fairy mischief!" she chirped.

From a quick walk through Monsterville, Darcy could see that the town was different. The fairies had transformed the place for their convention.

Main Street sparkled like a diamond field.

In the woods, giant mushrooms provided cozy beds for the countless visiting sprites.

Glitter Lake had been turned into a tropical sea. Palm trees ringed the water, waving in the warm breeze. Some monsters waded in the turquoise waters. Others surfed in the gentle waves that hit the pink beach.

And everywhere, fairies lit the air like fireflies on a summer night.

After a winter of snow and blustery winds, Darcy welcomed the warm wonderland. A toss of pixie dust had changed the kids from their snow gear to swimsuits, and the girls were about to dive into Glitter Lake.

Sam was on the other side of the lake, trying his hand at surfing. A couple of werewolves in flowered shorts were paddling out. And Vladu the vampire was hanging ten, his purple cape streaming behind him.

"Ooooh! The water's warm," Fiona said, hugging an inner tube with the head of a dragon.

"And look at the pink sand on the bottom," Darcy said, wiggling her toes.

"This is the life," Francie said, sinking back onto a squishy raft. "It's times like this I wonder why I ever wanted to become a girl."

Darcy blinked as the words stabbed at her heart. Her feet touched the sandy bottom as she turned to look at Francie. Did she mean it?

But Francie was already paddling off to the tiny island in the center of the lake.

Darcy swam until she was sure she'd turn into a mermaid if she stayed in the water one minute longer. As the girls were drying off, Fiona pointed out a group of monsters heading down the path.

"The werewolves said something about flying lessons," she said eagerly. "Can we go, too?"

"Sure." Francie took one more swipe at her hair with a thick towel, then pulled on a big flowered shirt.

"It's really nice of the fairies to whip up all these neat things for us," said Darcy. She pulled on long plaid shorts and a white tank top.

"Piece of cake," Francie said. "It's easy when you have fairy dust in your fingertips."

The girls followed the path through the woods. Through the trees Darcy could see an open meadow dotted with colorful wildflowers. Groups of fairies were lifting off from fat leaves, using their sparkling trails to tow monsters through the air.

"Wow! Dee is flying!" Fiona shouted, running ahead.

"Along with Ay, Bee, and Eff." Francie smiled as one of the yeti cubs landed in a pile of hay.

"They're so cute." The small bearlike creatures with human features reminded Darcy of teddy bears.

Fiona was already dancing through the field and greeting the yetis. The girls watched as a squadron of fairies lifted a zombie, sending him sailing over treetops.

"The view is s-s-spectacular!" the zombie sputtered as he gently dropped into a patch of clover.

"I want to fly again!" Dee said gleefully.

"I want to fly to the Arctic!" Ay added.

"Yeah! And we can visit Dad!" Dee agreed.

"I didn't know you had a father," Fiona said curiously. "How come I never met him?"

"He's been up north for a long time," Dee told her. "He's helping the Arctic yetis. But we really miss him."

"Who's next?" a yellow fairy called out.

"I want to go again!" Dee shouted.

A pink sprite darted over to the girls and asked, "Wanna take a spin, Francie girl?"

"I've done it a million times," Francie answered. "Give someone else a try."

"Me!" Fiona jumped up. "Me-me-me! Please?"

"Sure, kid," the yellow fairy said. She spun a web of yellow dust around Fiona's waist and gave it a test tug. Fiona was lifted off the ground, then dropped back to her feet.

"You're such a little thing, I can handle you on my own," said the yellow fairy.

"Careful, Daisy," the other fairy called.

"I can do it, Pinky." Daisy spun an extra line of pixie dust around Fiona's shoulders, then hoisted her into the air.

Fiona wiggled her legs happily as the ground rushed by beneath her. "I'm flying!"

"Way to go, Fee!" Darcy called as her cousin rose into the sky. The fairy rides looked fun.

But Francie wasn't as enthusiastic. "I hope Daisy is careful," she said, nibbling her lip. "It's not easy for one fairy to lift a person—even a little person."

At the edge of the woods, Fiona's feet were skimming over the crest of an evergreen. Daisy zigzagged, and Fee swung through the air, shouting, "This is the best! I feel as light as—"

Just then part of the web snapped, and Fiona slipped down a few feet. "Whoa!" she yelped.

"Oh my gosh!" Francie gasped.

A second later, the yellow web broke completely. . . .

And Fiona dropped straight into the woods!

"It's too awful!" Darcy gasped. She and Francie were racing toward the forest.

"It's my fault!" Francie called as she plunged into the woods. "I saw it coming. If only I still had my powers . . . I could've saved Fee."

Their eyes fixed on Daisy's blinking yellow light, they ran through the underbrush. Darcy's heart was thumping in her chest. Was Fiona okay? She'd fallen so far. . . .

At last they spotted Fiona, stretched out in a small clearing.

"Fee!" Francie shouted. "Are you okay?"

Darcy was right behind her. "We saw you—"

Just then Fiona bolted up with a huge smile on her face. "I'm fine," she chirped. "Look at this!" She nestled into the cushy cap of a giant mushroom. "I landed in a fairy bed. It made me bounce in the air like a trampoline!"

"Oh, Fee!" Darcy's heart lifted with relief.

"Scared me to death, I'll admit," Daisy said with a burst of yellow light. "That's the last time I'll ever try to tow someone alone."

"We were so worried about you," Francie said, ruffling Fiona's curly mop. "That was quite a fall."

"I *was* scared," Fiona admitted. "But it was fun flying." She turned her heart-shaped face up toward Daisy. "Can we do it again?"

"Are you nuts?" Darcy asked. "After what just happened—"

"That's enough flying for one day," Francie said firmly. She helped Fiona off the fat mushroom. "Let's find Sam."

🦇 🦇 🦇

"I wish we could've stayed in Monsterville for- ever. Or at least overnight," Fiona said as the kids skied through the still-falling snow. They were minutes from home. The wooden bridge over the frozen creek was just around the corner.

"No way," Darcy said. "Our parents would freak out if we were missing in a storm like this. Mom's laid down the rule: I have to be back in the neighborhood by the time it gets dark."

"Besides," Sam added, "how would you explain it to them. Just call them on the phone—if the monsters *had* phones—and tell them the truth? 'Hey, Mom, Dad, we're bunking in with a bunch of zombies and ghosts tonight.'"

The kids laughed.

"You're so smart, Sammy-lammy," Fiona said as Darcy and the others moved ahead of her on the trail. She paused and adjusted her mittens. "Hey, guys! Slow down!"

"Get your rear in gear!" Sam called back.

"But I'm tired," Fiona pleaded. She took a few steps, then stopped again. "You guys have longer legs. You can go faster."

Darcy paused and turned back. "Come on, Fee. It's going to be dark soon."

A crackling sound behind them made both girls turn around. The noise was coming from the woods.

Like a shot, Fiona skied ahead until she was beside Darcy. "Did you hear that?" she asked.

Darcy nodded. "Probably an animal looking for its dinner."

"Well, I don't want to be it," Fiona said. Her face was tight with fear.

As they skied a few more paces, Fiona began to lag behind again.

"Come on, Fee," Sam said impatiently. "We don't have all night."

"I'm going as fast as I can," she insisted. "But

I'm cold. And tired. And scared. Something is following us."

"Yeah, sure," Sam said sarcastically.

"Really!" Fee insisted. "Darcy heard it, too."

Darcy shrugged. "I did, Sam."

Sam stopped and pounded one ski into the snow. "You may have heard something, but it's *not* following us."

Sensing a fight, Darcy paused and knocked the packed snow off her ski poles.

"How do you know?" Fiona challenged Sam. "Why don't you just go on ahead. Leave me behind to be eaten by the Claw."

"Now, Fee . . ." Francie soothed her.

"Don't baby her," Sam ordered, "or she'll act like a baby."

"Will not!" Fiona exclaimed.

"I think we all need a break." Francie pulled off a mitten and reached into her pocket. "Let's have some granola bars."

"All right," Sam said, taking a bar. He looked up at the sky and frowned. "But let's get away from the snow and wind by scooting under that pine tree." He pointed to a towering evergreen with a wide skirt of solid white snow.

Darcy ducked under the lowest branches and slid into the dark, protected area. "This is kind of cozy," she said.

The kids huddled around the wide tree trunk. Hunkering down on their skis, they ripped into their snack packets.

"I'll take a break," Fiona said quietly. "But don't blame me when the Claw catches up with us."

"There's no such thing as the Claw," Sam said, rolling his eyes. "Sometimes you can be such a pest."

"I'm just telling you what I heard," Fiona said ominously.

"Let's not start fighting now, guys," Francie said. "We're almost home. Soon we'll be out of the snow and snuggled up in—"

Just then a noise sounded from nearby.

"There it is again," Darcy said. "Listen." It sounded like something was moving through the snow.

A curious look crossed Sam's face.

"So you hear it?" Darcy whispered.

"Told you," Fiona said smugly.

Francie popped the rest of her granola bar into her mouth. "Maybe we should—"

Suddenly snow began to fall in giant clumps as the tree rocked overhead.

Sam bolted up. "What the heck is that?"

"Grrr . . . ," came the low snarl.

A towering figure was shaking the skirt of the tree!

"Grrrr!" the thing growled.

"Aaaarrhhh!" the kids shrieked.

"Come on! Hurry!" Sam shouted.

The kids scrambled up, struggling to turn their skis around.

As Darcy pushed off the ground, she caught a glimpse of the creature. Its huge muzzle of teeth glistened in the shadows. It swaggered like a large man. That was no bear!

And right now, it was swaggering toward her.

Frantically, she sidestepped on her skis, but it was getting closer . . .

Closer!

It reached a long arm out, swiping at her chin, and Darcy's heart thudded in her chest.

Her eyes were glued to the long white paw . . .

A twisted claw with six-inch nails!

Adrenaline surged through Darcy's veins as she propelled her skis to the edge of the tree. Without daring to look back, she slid onto the fresh snow and pushed off. Seconds later she was back on the trail, on the heels of the other kids.

They hurried across the wooden bridge, then coasted down a hill. Even when the growling stopped, they kept pushing along. Luckily, Fiona managed to keep up.

Within minutes they were coasting into the pasture of the Ryan ranch. Nobody said a word until they were in the mudroom, stripping off their jackets and snow gear.

"Everybody okay?" Sam asked.

The kids nodded.

"I dropped my granola bar under that tree," Fiona whimpered.

"Don't worry," said Francie. "We'll get you something else to eat."

"Just be glad that creature didn't get any closer to you," Sam told his younger sister. He yanked her wool cap off and tousled her brown curls. "You would've been a tasty snack for that bear."

"I'm not so sure it *was* a bear," Darcy interrupted. She hung her jacket on a peg and turned to Sam. "Did you see how it walked? On two feet, just like a man."

"I know what you mean," Francie said, tugging off her scarf. "Bears have trouble walking upright. That creature walked on two legs with ease."

"Well, whatever it is, the sheriff should know about it," said Sam. "There's a wild animal loose in the woods. Sheriff Smoke can issue a warning or something."

He went off to make the call while the girls slipped off the rest of their snow gear and went into the living room. A warm fire was set, and the smell of baking chicken filled the air.

"Yum-yummy!" Fiona chirped.

"Is that my favorite niece?" Pam Ryan stuck her head out of the kitchen doorway.

"You're such a good cook, Aunt Pam," Fiona beamed. "I wish *we* were having chicken tonight."

"You are," Darcy's mother explained. "Your parents are on their way over. Seems the storm knocked all the electricity out at your place."

"Great!" Fiona said, rubbing her hands together.

"You kids better warm up by the fire," Pam Ryan said. "Once the potatoes are baking, I'll leave it to you to make a salad. And what's this I hear about a bear near the ranch?"

The girls told her about their encounter in the woods.

"Hmm." Pam Ryan's brows rose in concern. "A wild bear? He must have been very hungry to be out and about in this weather. Most grizzlies spend the colder months in semihibernation."

Darcy covered her mouth. "I forgot about that. . . ." Having grown up on a Montana ranch, she knew a lot about bears.

"Oh, well," her mom added. "You kids had better be extra careful when you're out in those woods. You don't want to startle or corner the poor thing."

When Darcy's mother went off to change out of her work clothes, the girls huddled around the fire.

"There's something weird about that bear," said Darcy.

"Did you see its fur?" Fiona asked. "It was white as snow."

"Maybe it's a white grizzly," Francie said.

"But there's something else," Darcy added. "When I turned back—"

"Well," Sam interrupted, coming in and plopping down on the sofa. "That's settled."

"Did you report the bear?" asked Fiona.

Sam nodded. "Sheriff Smoke promised to get a warning out to local skiers and hunters."

"Hunters," Fiona huffed. "I hate hunters."

"It's a fact of life, Fee," Sam explained.

"Shooting an innocent bear?" Fiona folded her arms over her chest. "Might as well rip my teddy bear to shreds."

"Still, people should be warned," Francie said sternly. "Bears can be dangerous."

Darcy nodded. "They hate to be cornered. And they can hurt you quicker than you can blink. Did you know that a grizzly bear has forty-two teeth?"

"Well, Sheriff Smoke is going to search the woods for our grizzly," Sam said.

"I don't think it was a bear," said Fiona. "I think we ran into the Claw."

"Get out," Sam said. "I didn't hear it growl, *Beware the Claw.*"

"But . . . about that legend," said Darcy. She cast an uneasy glance at Fiona, then went on. "When I was hurrying away, I caught a look at its right paw. It was . . . well, sort of twisted. And it had really long nails. Like . . . at least six inches!"

🦇 🦇 🦇

It took most of the night for the other kids to calm Fiona down. She was sure that they'd had a run-in with the Claw.

Charles and Lila Mackie seemed to think the kids were exaggerating. Still, they repeated the warning Darcy's mom had given them: Stay away from the bear!

As she slid under the covers that night, Darcy wasn't sure what to think. Maybe the long winter of snow had driven the Claw out, after all these years.

Whatever the creature was, one thing was for sure.

It wasn't very friendly.

By Sunday morning the snow had stopped. Darcy finished off her homework after breakfast and offered to help her mom with chores.

"Well, the horses could use some exercise," Pam Ryan said, reaching for the Sunday paper. "With all this snow, they've been cooped up in the barn."

"I'll give you a hand," Francie offered as she loaded a plate into the dishwasher. "I wanted to bring these scraps out to Thunder." Francie had developed a special relationship with Thunder, a jet-black stallion who often gave ranch hands a hard time.

An hour later, the girls were outside the barn, their breath forming puffs in the cold air. The snow had stopped, and the sun was warm and bright. They took turns bridling the horses and leading them around the corral, being extra careful to avoid the deeper snowdrifts.

Darcy was just taking her favorite colt, Gingersnap, out of the stable when Fiona joined them. She was bundled in a down jacket and pulled her blue sled.

"It's boring at our house," Fiona complained. "Mom and Dad are reading the paper. And Sam is tutoring Jake Milridge in gem-a-tree."

"That's *geometry,*" Darcy corrected.

"How about helping us?" Francie suggested. "These horses need extra attention."

Fiona reached up and patted Gingersnap with a mittened hand. "I can do that," she said, pressing her nose to the colt's flank. "Let's take a walk, you cutesy-wootsy!"

The girls were walking Gingersnap around the corral when they noticed two figures bobbing up the hill.

"Look!" Fiona pointed toward the trail. "Someone's going into the woods."

Darcy strained for a better look. "Not just someone. That's Annabel Mackinac and Torie Pollack."

"Ugh!" Francie groaned. Annabel was in

Darcy's class at school, but everyone in town knew she was a total bully. "What's Queen Annabel doing in our neck of the woods?"

Just then Annabel noticed the girls in the corral. She tugged on Torie's sleeve, and they approached.

"Looks like we're going to find out," Darcy said. She handed Gingersnap's reins to Francie, who led the colt into the barn.

"Hey, Darcy," Annabel whined. Under her white beret, her blond hair hung in perfect curls to her waist. She lifted a black video camera to her face, adding, "Smile for the camera."

"Very funny," Darcy said, brushing her sweaty bangs under her wool cap.

"Is that thing on?" Fiona asked with a sweet smile.

"Not right now," Annabel admitted.

"We're saving our tape for the best shots of the Claw," Torie added. "Annabel and I are going to capture the creature on tape."

"Good luck," Darcy said in a sour voice. "No one has seen him for years."

"But Darcy—" Fiona tugged on Darcy's arm, but Darcy ignored her. She hated Annabel's smug attitude.

"Liar, liar, pants on fire," Annabel crowed. "We

know you're fibbing. Sheriff Smoke told Torie's dad all about yesterday."

Torie nodded. "So don't try to hide the story from us. We know you know."

"Maybe we saw a bear," Darcy began.

"But Darcy—" Fiona interrupted again.

"Just a white grizzly," Darcy continued as Francie reappeared by her side.

"What do you want the tape for?" Francie asked. "A school project?"

"Who cares about school?" Annabel flashed them a white smile. "My dad knows the producer of 'Outrageous Videos.' If we can get this beast on tape, Dad will rush it to the producer." She tossed her platinum hair. "We're bound to win producer of the week."

"They'll fly us out to Hollywood," Torie added, grinning at Fiona. "You can watch us on TV."

"Wow," Fiona breathed.

Darcy nudged her cousin. Had she forgotten the lousy things Annabel had done to them over the years?

"So . . . ," Annabel said. "Got any hot tips for us?"

"Sorry," Darcy said glumly. "All I can say is, be careful. You know how dangerous bears can be."

"You don't scare us," Annabel said, turning away.

"Really," Torie parroted.

As the girls strode off, Darcy felt her face growing hot. Oooh, they burned her up.

"Why didn't you tell them about the Claw?" Fiona asked.

"Because I'm not sure it *is* the Claw out there," Darcy said. "And because they don't deserve our help."

"I wish they took a shot of me," Fiona said sadly.

Just then they heard a happy cry from the trail. Torie and Annabel were bending over, staring at something on the ground.

"They must've found a clue," Francie said.

"They're going to be mincemeat," Darcy added. She hopped the fence and headed up the hill. Much as she disliked Annabel, she didn't want to think about what that bear might do to her.

By the time Darcy, Francie, and Fiona reached the hilltop, the camera was rolling.

"These are footprints from the Claw," Annabel narrated for the videotape.

Darcy knelt down and studied the tracks. They looked like bear prints . . . sort of. Five toes, five claws, but a much longer foot than a bear. Each print was at least a foot and a half long!

"And the prints lead into the woods, where the Claw was last spotted." Annabel's voice dripped with mystery. "Let's take a look. . . ."

Ignoring the camera, Darcy pushed past the two girls and followed the tracks. The creature must have followed them to the ranch last night!

Darcy paced beside the prints until she came to a second trail—tiny red dots in the snow. . . .

A trail of blood.

"Blood!" Behind Darcy, Francie whispered the word.

"Is the Claw hurt?" Fiona asked.

"Either that or he's hurt someone else," said Darcy.

Francie's green eyes focused on the red stains, and then she shuddered. "Let's go back to the ranch," she said, her hand on Darcy's shoulder. "We'd better report this to Sheriff Smoke."

Seeing Annabel and Torie coming down the trail, Darcy paused. "I know you'll think I'm nuts," she said under her breath. "But I'm afraid to leave those two thimble-heads alone in the woods. What if they become the Claw's next victims?"

"So you *do* believe in the Claw," Fiona said. "I knew it."

Francie looked back at the girls. "What do you want to do?" she asked Darcy.

"I don't know," Darcy said, nibbling her lower

lip. "Maybe if we keep an eye on them?"

"Okay," Francie agreed. "Let's just hope they don't do anything stupid."

"Hmph," Darcy grunted.

"We can pretend we're spies working on a big case," Fiona suggested. She ducked behind a tree stump near the edge of the trail. "I love secret stuff."

Darcy tried to act casual as they followed the two girls down the path. They had to stop every few steps and listen as Annabel barked orders like, "Hold the camera steady!" and "Make sure I'm in the shot!"

Sometimes Darcy wondered how Torie could stand to be friends with Annabel Mackinac.

Annabel and Torie didn't seem to care that they were being followed. That was one thing about Annabel—she loved an audience.

When the tracks reached the creek, they suddenly disappeared. Annabel paused, rubbing her chin with a fat mitten.

"Bummer!" Annabel pointed to the snow at her feet. "The Claw's footprints end at this bridge. But that doesn't mean that he didn't cross it. The snow's just packed really hard here."

Darcy stared down at the snow. Annabel was right about one thing: There'd been a lot of traffic on this bridge. Leaning over the rail,

Darcy's eyes lit on the frozen creek. It was covered with snow . . . and a clue!

Annabel led Torie—and the camera—across the bridge. "We'll pick up the Claw's prints on the other side." Flashing a wicked grin at the camera, she added: "Let's hope he hasn't gobbled up a skier for breakfast."

Francie and Fiona started across the bridge, but Darcy hung back at the wooden rail.

"Darcy?" Francie called back. "Are you coming?"

Darcy shook her head.

Fiona's brows knitted in confusion. "But I thought you wanted to—"

Seeing that Annabel and Torie were a safe distance away, Darcy explained, "If they keep going off in that direction, they'll be safe from the creature."

"How do you know?" asked Francie.

Darcy pointed down at the frozen creek. "Footprints."

Francie leaned over the rail and gasped. "Not just *any* prints. That's definitely our bear!"

Darcy nodded. "It must have hopped off the bridge and walked along the frozen creek."

"It's pretty clever," Francie said.

Fiona scratched her head through her wool cap. "I wonder how far the tracks go?"

Just then a distant buzz echoed through the woods. Frightened, Fiona grabbed Francie's jacket

44

and huddled closer. "Is that . . . the Claw?"

Darcy laughed. "Only if he's riding a snow-mobile." She listened closely, then added, "A bunch of snowmobiles, headed in this direction."

The girls waited on the bridge until the vehicles came into sight on the trail. It was a group of hunters, their rifle bags slung over their shoulders. Darcy had seen one man at school. He was the father of one of the kids in her class, Jordan Black.

"Hey, girls," one of the hunters said. "Don't wander too far into the woods."

"This is a dangerous area, Darcy. We just got a message from Sheriff Smoke," Mr. Black said. He pointed to his cellular phone. "The Claw has been spotted nearby."

"Are you sure?" Darcy asked. "Or was that just Annabel Mackinac making up stories?"

"Now why would somebody do that?" asked another hunter.

"Because she wants to be on TV," Fiona said simply. "She's been out here with her friend Torie videotaping the Claw's tracks. She followed its trail into the woods over there." She pointed into the forest.

"Two girls, alone in the woods." Mr. Black rubbed his eyes wearily. "We'd better go find them."

"But what about the beast?" another hunter asked, hugging his rifle.

"It may be right on their heels." Mr. Black revved the engine of his snowmobile. Waving to the girls, he sped over the bridge. The other hunters zoomed off behind him.

Francie flashed Darcy a curious expression. "Want to explain that?"

"Darcy hates the hunters, too," Fiona said gleefully. "That's why she sent them off in the wrong direction."

Darcy shrugged. "That and the fact that I can't wait to see Annabel get in trouble for ignoring the sheriff's warning." She shoved her hands into her pockets. "I guess we should head back."

"But it's still early," Fiona said, leaning over the bridge rail. "Can't we follow the Claw's footprints and see where they lead?"

Francie hesitated. "The sheriff warned us. . . ."

"And so did our parents," Darcy added. Still, she had to admit she was a little bit curious about the creature. What *was* a bear doing out in weather like this? And the blood . . . Was it injured? Was it dying?

"What if we follow the footprints?" Darcy suggested. "Just for a few minutes. We won't go too far from home."

The three girls exchanged a look. Fiona grinned, and Darcy felt a little thrill inside her chest.

Francie shook her head, a wry look in her green eyes. "Something tells me I'm going to regret this," she said as she headed down the shallow creek bank.

The girls followed the frozen brook until the tracks led off along the embankment. This end of the creek was quiet, far from the trail. They checked the area for clues, but the prints ended at the base of a pine tree.

"That's strange," Francie said, kneeling down to search the ground.

"At least there's no more blood," said Darcy. She lifted a tree branch and spotted a dark, circular object underneath. "Look at this."

Francie moved closer. It was a bed of fresh pine needles. Reaching out to touch it, Francie said, "It looks like a nest for—"

"Aaargh!" Fiona's shriek cut through the air.

Her heart in her throat, Darcy twisted around and saw it. . . .

The Claw.

The huge creature was holding Fiona by the collar of her ski parka. Swinging helplessly in the air, she looked like a little rag doll.

"Help!" she cried, her face wet with tears as the creature lowered her to his muzzle.

Darcy saw a flash of sharp, gleaming teeth as the creature opened its mouth.

The Claw was getting ready to bite into Fiona's neck!

Darcy's blood turned to ice at the horrible sight. There was no time to think. No time to plan.

"Stop!" she shouted, lunging at the creature.

The distraction made the beast hesitate.

She seized the moment and pounded on his bear paw with her heavy snow boot.

"Eeeeow!" the creature howled.

At the same time, Francie reached up and tore Fiona out of his grasp. The girls stumbled backward as the giant, furry beast grabbed its sore toe and let out another yelp of pain.

"Come on," Darcy gasped, pulling the other girls to their feet. They were skidding down the frozen creek when the creature growled again.

"You didn't have to do that!" it rasped in a low, scratchy voice. "Especially with those ten-ton boots on."

The kids wheeled around and stared.

It talked!

From a safe distance Darcy studied the creature's face. Its fuzzy face was weathered and dried, but there was something familiar about the eyes . . . and all that white fur.

"It's not a bear," Francie said under her breath.

"And it's not the Claw," said Fiona. Her fear gave way to a calmness. "You're a yeti, aren't you?"

The creature's eyes closed and he sighed, as if he were very tired. "Yes," he whispered.

Darcy was confused. He looked different from the others. He was so *huge*! His face was fuzzier. And his skin was cracked and brown, while the other yetis had soft, pink faces.

"How come you don't look like Dee or Ay?" Fiona asked. "Or even Marta?"

A spark of recognition glimmered in his eyes. "You know them?" He stepped toward the girls eagerly.

Francie nodded. "They're our friends," she said firmly. She slipped an arm over Fiona's shoulders and pulled her into the crook of her arm. "*They* would never attack us."

"I'm sorry," he said, staring down at the frozen ground. "I wouldn't have hurt you. Honestly, I was just trying to scare you away. People are a danger to me."

Fiona put her hands on her hips. "A big bear like you?"

"Even *I* can't stop a bullet." His twisted paw reached up toward his neck and pushed a matted section of fur away.

Darcy's stomach tightened when she saw the wound. The fur on his shoulder was dark with dried blood.

"You were shot?" asked Darcy.

He shook his head. "Wood chips. A hunter's bullet ricocheted off a tree."

"Does it hurt?" Fiona asked.

He grumbled. "Not too bad. But I can't reach it to clean it out. And the blood keeps attracting predators."

And us, thought Darcy, remembering how they'd noticed the blood trail in the woods.

Francie eyed him thoughtfully. "Why are you living out in the woods—especially during a storm?"

"I was just passing through when I got wounded," he explained. "I'm trying to get back to my family. My wife, Marta, and my cubs, Ay, Bee, Cee, Dee—"

"You mean—" Fiona's eyes lit with excitement.

"*You're* their father?" Darcy asked.

When the creature nodded, Fiona clapped her hands. "Yippee! Dee's going to be so excited. And Gee. And Ay. This is going to be great!"

The yetis' father! Darcy could hardly believe it.

Dee had mentioned that his father was working up in the Arctic, but she'd never expected to run into him in the woods.

"You know," Fiona told him, "everyone in Whiterock thinks you're the Claw."

"Well . . ." His weathered lips formed a smile. "Actually, Claw *is* my name. I used to have quite a reputation in these parts when I was younger."

"You mean, the legend is true?" asked Darcy.

"I scared off a few hunters in my day," he admitted. "But I don't know what got everyone all stirred up around here today."

"I do," Francie said quietly. "When we ran into you last night, we were a little shaken. We thought you were a bear. Our friend, Sam, called the sheriff to get the word out."

Claw let out a moan. "No wonder the woods have been hopping today." Discouraged, he reached for his wounded shoulder. He had started to bleed again. "I'm never going to get through this forest."

"We know the way to Monsterville," Fiona offered. "We could help you."

"But it's a good hike," Francie added. "And we'll never be able to avoid everyone who's trying to track you down."

Darcy thought of the hunters, the sheriff, and Annabel and Torie and their camera. Claw was definitely a hunted creature.

"Nope," Darcy told him. "You'll never make it to Monsterville today. But you can't stay here, either."

"Not after Bigmouth Sam called the sheriff," Fiona added. "What're we going to do?"

Darcy looked from her friends to the big wounded yeti. "Come home with us," she said. "I live on a ranch, not far from here. You can rest there."

"We'll get you bandaged up," Francie offered.

"And I'll make you some hot cocoa," Fiona chimed in.

"I don't know," he said hesitantly. "I really need to get home. . . ."

"But you'll never make it there today," Darcy insisted. "We'll get you back on the trail tomorrow. I'm sure things will have died down by then, especially if nobody sees you out here today."

Claw rubbed his furry forearms over his fuzzy, wrinkled face. Darcy could see that he was exhausted. "I appreciate your kindness," he said. "Lead on."

"This is gonna be great," Fiona said, taking him by the paw. "I'd love to see Dee's face when he gets a look at you!"

🦇 🦇 🦇

"That's the barn," Darcy said, pointing through a snow-covered vine, "the red building."

The trip back had been a little scary, with the

buzz of snowmobiles echoing in the air. The girls couldn't tell if it was the pack of hunters or just tourists, but they'd hung back just the same. If one person got a look at Claw, the woods would be swarming for days.

"All we have to do is get past that stretch by the paddock," Francie said.

"We can walk along the fence," Darcy suggested. "It's covered with snow, and you can barely see through it."

"Good idea," Francie said.

They moved through the frozen underbrush until they reached the outside of the Ryans' property line. The walk along the fence was easy enough. And when they reached the barn, Darcy was relieved to find that the side door was unlocked.

But as soon as they opened the door, trouble began.

The barn cats began to screech as if they were being tortured. Fatso leaped down from the hayloft and hissed at the kids and their new friend.

Fiona reached down to pet Jasper, but the feline arched its back and snarled.

"Fatso! Skunky! Stop that!" Darcy snapped at the cats.

But the cats wouldn't obey. And as Francie closed the door behind them, the horses began to act up, too.

"What's wrong with them?" Fiona asked.

"It must be Claw's scent," Darcy said. "It's making the animals nervous."

Thunder kicked in his stall. Gingersnap whinnied and stamped her hooves. The other horses were skittish, stamping and bucking against the boards.

"This will never work," Claw said miserably.

"Calm down!" Darcy shouted to the animals.

In response, they stirred even more.

Just then Thunder reared up. A second later, he kicked with his rear legs, and Darcy heard a board crack.

The stallion was trying to break out of his stall!

Darcy's eyes widened. "We can't stay here," she said. "The horses are totally freaked out."

"But where are we going to go?" Francie asked. "Claw isn't safe in the woods."

Darcy turned to the yeti, who was shrinking back toward the door. Where in the world could you hide a six-foot, furry creature with claws?

"Let's take him to my house!" Fiona crowed. Her eyes lit up as the idea took shape. "We can keep him in the shed in the backyard. I'll feed him and take care of him, and nobody will ever know he's there."

Francie and Darcy exchanged a look.

"It's not a bad idea," Francie admitted.

"Except that you live in town," Darcy added. "We'll never be able to sneak Claw through Whiterock."

Francie came up behind Darcy and tugged off

her wool cap. "Never say never," she said. She took Darcy's hat over and plopped it onto Claw's head. "If we tuck in the fur and use a muffler . . ."

"A disguise!" Fiona said. "I *love* dressing up."

"What about his face?" Darcy asked. "And *no* kid is six feet tall." She wasn't quite sure about Francie's plan.

"We'll get one of your mom's ski masks," Francie said. "And we'll pull him on Fiona's sled. With his legs covered, people will just think he's a big kid."

Fiona danced over to Claw and wrapped her scarf around his neck. "There you go!" she crowed.

"I don't think I'm going to like this," Claw said. He loosened the muffler.

"Trust me," Francie said with a grin. "I have an eye for fashion."

🦇 🦇 🦇

Ten minutes later, they were on their way. Covered in snow gear and a big orange poncho the girls had found in the tack room, Claw looked . . . well, as Francie put it, "Winter wear extraordinaire."

Darcy slowed her steps to maneuver the sled around a corner. She and Francie had decided to take turns pulling, and it was a good thing. Claw was heavy. But at least they'd reached the paved street, where the snow along the shoulder was packed down from foot traffic.

"Wait till Sam gets a load of you," Fiona told Claw. "He's scared of dogs. One look at you and he'll run like crazy."

"Great," Claw muttered. "Something else to look forward to."

"Maybe we should keep Claw a secret for a while," Francie suggested. "The last thing we need is a lot of commotion at your house, Fee."

"A secret?" Fiona grinned. "I *love* secrets."

"Then maybe you'll be able to keep this one," Darcy said firmly. Fiona was not very good in the secrets department. Usually you could count on her to spill the beans.

They were getting closer to town, and the streets were sectioned off into blocks lined with trees and houses.

"My turn," Francie said, taking over the sled rope. "You look beat," she told Darcy.

Darcy's arms were tired. *But not as tired as Claw must be,* she thought as she walked alongside the yeti. Under the snow gear he was sagging, nearly dropping off to sleep.

"You'll be able to sleep when we get to the Mackies' house," Darcy told him.

"I just need a nap," he said quietly. "Something to tide me over. Just a little more strength to get me home to Monsterville. It'll be so good to be back."

As they passed a group of kids building a snowman, Darcy realized how much she'd miss Whiterock if she had to go away.

"How long were you away from home?" she asked Claw.

"Five years," he said. "My cubs were still babies. I would never have left them, but it was for family. My mother's brood were having trouble with Arctic hunters. I had to show them how to avoid danger so they could survive."

Five years . . . Darcy couldn't imagine being away from her mom for so long. And it was hard to remember how things were before the Mackies moved from Chicago—or before Francie had come to live at the ranch. Although they'd come to Whiterock just months ago, they were already family.

"Oooomph!" Francie grunted, pulling the sled onto the Mackies' block. "It's times like these when I really miss that pixie dust. Muscle power just doesn't cut it."

"We're almost there," Fiona chirped, reaching down to adjust Claw's hat. "Then we'll have hot cocoa and a nice, cozy shed."

"That sounds wonderful," Claw said with a yawn.

Her boots crunching on the packed snow,

Darcy glanced toward Fiona's house . . .

And froze in her tracks.

"Oh my gosh!" she gasped.

A black police Jeep was parked smack in front of the Mackies' house.

And standing on the front porch was Sheriff Smoke!

The other girls gasped as they caught sight of the sheriff.

"Quick!" Fiona whispered. "Cut through the side yard. Before he turns ar—"

But it was too late. The sheriff had already wheeled around on the porch and spotted the girls.

"Hey!" He waved. Before the girls could move he was jogging over.

He's coming! Darcy thought frantically. She shot a look at Claw. He was hunched over, napping. But a thatch of white fur poked out from his neck. She swooped down and tugged the scarf over it just as the sheriff approached.

"Just the girls I was looking for," he said with a friendly smile. "Ken Black radioed in that he spotted you in the woods. Right around the area where that attack occurred."

"Yes, sir," Francie said with a serious expression.

The sheriff's dark eyes were full of concern. "Well, I'm glad you're okay. But you were warned about going into the woods."

"Annabel Mackinac and Torie Pollack went there first," Fiona blabbed. "*We* were just trying to keep *them* out of trouble."

"Is that so?" the sheriff said quietly.

"Did Mr. Black mention them?" Darcy asked. "I mean, they made it out okay, right?"

The tall man nodded. There was something about Sheriff Smoke—his quiet manner and dark, perceptive eyes—that made Darcy want to trust him. At least, more than she trusted most adults. But he *was* the town sheriff. And at the moment they were trying to smuggle the infamous Claw right under his nose.

"Annabel and Torie are safe at home," the sheriff said, his eyes skimming over the bundle on the sled. "And who's this?"

"He's our new friend," Fiona chirped.

"That's some outfit," Sheriff Smoke observed.

"Francie helped pick it out," Fiona reported.

Darcy wanted to stick a sock in her cousin's mouth. This was one time when being a chatterbox wasn't handy.

As the sheriff glanced down at the sled, Claw shifted in his sleep, kicking the poncho aside. It gaped open, revealing a slit of white fur.

Darcy's heart was in her throat. They were doomed! The sheriff's jaw dropped as he noticed the white pelt.

"It's the Petersons' dog," Francie croaked, covering quickly. "We . . . um, found him wandering around the ranch, and . . . um . . ."

"And the dog seemed cold," Darcy said, picking up the thread of the story. "So we dressed it up in snow gear."

The sheriff reached down and stroked Claw's flank. "That's some coat he's got there. Very healthy."

Darcy sank with relief. He was buying their story. At least for now. She petted Claw's head. "Yes, sir. This doggy loves his kibble."

"The Petersons are lucky you're taking such good care of him." The sheriff straightened as the radio in his Jeep started squawking. "I'd better get going. But you girls remember my warning. Steer clear of the woods till the commotion dies down."

Swallowing hard, Darcy nodded. "Yes, sir."

The girls waved as the sheriff jogged back to his Jeep and drove off.

"That was close," Fiona said. "He sure asks a lot of questions."

Then Francie tugged the sled toward the Mackies' side yard. "Come on," she said. "Before someone else comes along!"

The shed in the Mackies' backyard was used to store tools and the lawn mower. Fiona snitched a blanket from inside the house, and the girls set up an old beach chair for their patient. Using the Mackies' first aid kit, Francie cleaned Claw's wound and bandaged it up. Darcy made hot cocoa for all of them in the microwave. And she and Fiona managed to smuggle out carrots and a box of Wheaties without Lila Mackie noticing.

"It's not much," Darcy said, "but it'll help build up your strength."

"Delicious," Claw said, tossing back a handful of Wheaties. He snuggled up with the blue plaid blanket. "Thank you for everything."

He yawned, and Francie patted his arm before picking up the first aid kit. "You'll be able to sleep in here. The Mackies don't have any animals who might sniff you out."

"Nope," Fiona said sadly. "Sam doesn't like dogs. And Mom won't let me have a cat till I'm ten." She gave Claw a little hug. "Sleep tight."

"We'll help you get back to the woods as soon as school lets out," Darcy promised. She didn't want to think about the sheriff's warning. Besides, all they needed to do was to get Claw back on the path. He could find the way from there.

By tomorrow night, Claw would be safe at home in Monsterville.

🦇 🦇 🦇

"Guess I'd better scrub up those pots," Pam Ryan said, folding the last of the laundry.

Darcy looked up from the floor, where she was stretched out in front of the fire reading a book. Running a ranch was a lot of work. Sometimes it seemed like her mom never got a break.

"All done," Francie said, shuffling out of the kitchen in her bear slippers and sweats.

"Really?" Darcy's mother blinked and picked up the laundry basket. "Thanks, Francie. You're an angel."

Close, Darcy thought, smiling to herself. Her mother didn't know about Francie's past as a pixie.

On the way to the hall, Pam stopped at the wide picture window and pulled the curtain aside. "Oh, dear. It's snowing again. Just what we *don't* need," she said glumly.

"I love the snow," Francie said cheerfully. "It makes everything look clean and new."

"But right now it's threatening our barn," Mrs. Ryan said. "See the way it's piled up on the roof? That snow is very heavy. It won't take much more to make the roof buckle and collapse."

Darcy rolled over and sat up. She remembered

how the Whitmans' barn roof had caved in two winters ago. Some of the livestock had been killed. And right now Gingersnap was asleep in the barn, nestled up against her mother.

"What can we do, Mom?" she asked.

"We just have to wait it out," Pam Ryan said. She hoisted up the laundry basket and headed down the hall. "Pray that those beams hold."

Darcy went over to the window, where Francie was watching the lacy snowflakes.

"Pretty scary, huh?" Francie asked.

Darcy looped her arm through her friend's and nodded. For a few minutes they stared out, watching the lights of the barn glimmer in the falling snow.

How could something so pretty be so dangerous? Darcy wondered.

She blinked as the snowflakes seemed to wink back at her. Twinkling, sparkling, shining in bursts of orange, purple, and blue.

Wait a minute, Darcy thought. *Colored snowflakes?*

"Do you see them?" Francie said quietly.

"The fairies?" Darcy asked. "What are they doing here?"

The bursts of light grew brighter as the small squadron zipped closer to the house.

"I have a feeling we're going to find out,"

Francie said. She unlocked the window and cracked it open. A moment later, on a wave of cold air, the three fairies blew into the room.

"Whew!" Beryl said, landing on the window seat. "We almost didn't make it this time. Who's the wise guy who forecast clear skies?"

"It wasn't *supposed* to start snowing again," Hoshi insisted. "My pixie dust is strong, but I can't fix the weather."

"Quit complaining," Neona snapped. "It's not as if we could afford to wait around till morning."

"What's the rush?" Francie said. "You guys act like you're on a mission or something."

"We are," Hoshi said. She hovered before Francie's face, her hands on her hips. "We've got a mission. And *you're* our subject."

"What?" Francie's mouth dropped open.

Beryl glowed like a neon blueberry. "For our good deed, we're going to make you a fairy again."

"Pack your bags, Francie-pantsie," Neona said. "We've come to take you back!"

Darcy's heart sank down to her toes. Her worst nightmare was coming true!

"Take me back?" Francie could barely say the words. "I like it here just fine."

"Cut the martyr act," Neona said sharply.

"No need to put on a happy face for us," Hoshi added. "We got the message the other day."

"When you said that you missed being a fairy," Beryl explained. "And that you wish you still had your powers."

"Wait a minute," Francie said, her face turning pink. "I know I said that, but what I meant was—"

"You were the first one we thought of when we got the assignment," Neona interrupted. "As part of the workshop, we have to do a major good deed. *Before midnight.*"

"Midnight! Can you believe it!" Hoshi chirped.

"Of course, we knew we needed to work on some-one close by."

"So here we are," Beryl said. "Ready to go?"

"First of all," Francie began, "I turned into a girl because of a witch's spell."

"Tough stuff, I know," Hoshi said with a flash of purple. "But we figure if we combine our powers, and use extra pixie dust, and—"

"Enough talk," Neona said, weaving an orange web around Francie's shoulders. "We're on the clock, kids."

Francie's green eyes filled with alarm as the three fairies swooped down on her. "But I said that—"

"Oooh! I love fulfilling dreams," Beryl said, rubbing her hands together.

"Wait!" Darcy said, waving Neona away from her friend. "You can't take Francie away. She belongs here. My mom and I, we . . . we love her. She's part of our family now."

The fairies paused in midair.

"What's with Goldilocks?" Neona asked, nod-ding at Darcy.

Francie pulled the orange web off and slipped an arm over Darcy's shoulders. "She's my sister now," she said. "And this *is* where I belong. I appreciate the good deed, but I can't accept."

Disappointed, the fairies settled onto the arm of the sofa. "We're sunk," Beryl said.

"No, you're not," said Darcy. "It's not even nine o'clock. You still have three hours to do your good deed."

"But this isn't our territory," Neona whined.

"We don't know anyone around here," Hoshi explained. "And since we got here late, the other fairies had a head start scoping out Whiterock. All the people who need help are already taken."

"Not everyone," Francie said, her green eyes flashing. "I know a tremendous good deed. A stupendous deed. The best one in Whiterock. Just let me get my jacket."

Jacket? Darcy was confused. Was Francie going with them, after all? "Where are you going?" she asked as Francie returned, zipped up to the chin in her pink parka.

"Don't worry, Darce," she said with a huge grin. "I'm just going to get them started. I'll be back in a snap."

"Is this an outdoor errand?" Beryl asked as she flew to the door behind Francie. "I just got over that darned cold, and I don't want to catch another one."

"Whine, whine, whine," Neona griped.

"This feels great," Francie said. "I do miss all the good deeds we used to perform."

"Come on, girls!" Hoshi said with a burst of purple. "We've got work to do!"

"Holy cow!" Pam Ryan nearly dropped her coffee mug as she looked out the window the next morning. "What in the world . . . ?"

"What's wrong, Mom?" Darcy picked up her knapsack and ran over to her mother's side.

"The barn . . . ," Pam Ryan said, still staring. "It's . . . the snow is gone."

Darcy peered out. Except for a light dusting, the barn roof was clean. The huge mound of snow that had been weighing it down was gone.

"Wow!" Darcy crowed. "That's great! What happened?"

"I don't know," her mother said, biting her lip. "Sometimes loud noises like explosions cause the snow to crack and slide off . . . but I didn't hear anything last night. Did you?"

"No," Darcy answered. She was quiet for a minute, thinking. Then she grinned. The fairies.

"Well, who am I to question a miracle," Pam said. She smiled, then headed out to the kitchen, adding, "It's a *huge* relief."

Francie appeared in the hallway, tying her ginger hair back in a scrunchy. "She noticed?" she asked Darcy under her breath. "About the barn roof?"

Darcy nodded. "You could've told me that was what you guys were up to."

"I wanted it to be a surprise," Francie said with an impish grin. "Not bad for an old fairy, huh?"

"It's the best," said Darcy. "You still have your magic touch."

It was snowing again when Darcy and Francie caught the bus to school. As Darcy hopped off in front of the elementary school, she spotted Nora Chambers waving from the sidewalk. Nora had dark hair and a sprinkling of freckles. She was one of Darcy's best friends.

"Darcy! At last!" Nora called. "I thought you'd never get here."

As usual, Nora was bursting with news.

"Hey, Nora," Darcy said. "How was your weekend?"

"You'll never believe what happened to Brook this weekend," Nora said breathlessly. "Wait'll you hear! I mean, she's not here to tell you. But I am! Brook called me last night from the resort and her family is snowbound."

"Whoa!" Darcy grinned. "Snowed in at a ski resort! She's so lucky."

"And we have a boring old math test. And history. And science."

"It's not fair," Darcy said, linking her arm through Nora's. "But at least we're in this together."

"Good thing," Nora said as they turned toward the school. "I mean, at least we can suffer together.

And I'd die if I had to sit next to Jay Greenberg! And did you hear what Torie Pollack and Annabel Mackinac did this weekend?"

All day the fifth grade was buzzing with news of Annabel's video. She told kids that she had caught the Claw on tape, which burned Darcy up.

That Annabel was such a liar!

That afternoon, their teacher assigned a new history project. "You can choose between two things," Ms. Yellowfeather said. "Write and perform a play about the Declaration of Independence. Or rent the movie 1776 and write a report on it."

Darcy perked up. Did somebody say movie?

She signed up to watch the movie, while Nora joined a group that wanted to do a play.

"This is going to be super fun," she told Darcy. "Why don't you get in our group?"

"No, thanks," Darcy said. "I've always wanted to see this movie," she added. The real truth was that she couldn't spare the time after school to write and rehearse today. She had to get Claw out of Whiterock and back to the woods.

* * *

After school, the three girls met at the Mackies' shed. By the time Darcy got there, Claw was pacing around, already dressed in the poncho and Darcy's wool cap.

"Ready to go?" he asked, pulling on the ski mask. "I can't wait to see Marta and the cubs."

"Let's do it!" Fiona said.

Claw climbed on the sled, and Francie tucked the blue plaid blanket over his legs. "After what happened with Sheriff Smoke yesterday, we can't take any chances," she said.

Darcy dragged the sled for the first half of the trip. Claw was still heavy, but she didn't mind. After a good night's sleep and some food, he was a stronger, happier yeti.

In half an hour they were crossing the pasture behind the Ryan ranch. Up ahead the woods loomed, the trees sparkling like sugar towers.

"Almost there," Fiona said, trudging through the snow. "But I don't want you to go. It was fun having you out in the shed. Way better than having a dog."

"Thanks," Claw said. "But I've got to get back to my family."

"We'll see you next time we visit Monsterville," Darcy promised as Francie pulled the sled to a halt.

"How do you kids know about Monsterville?" Claw asked. "I thought it was well hidden in the mountains."

"It's a long story," Francie said, searching the path. "Looks like the coast is clear. Good luck, Claw. And tell the monsters we said hi."

"Bye, girls." His weathered lips formed a

grateful smile. He reached forward and gave them all a giant bear hug that nearly stole Darcy's breath away. . . .

And then he was on his way, lumbering down the path with a wide gait.

"Bye . . . ," the girls called softly. They watched him walk down toward the wooden bridge. His fur was so white, he blended in well with the snowy surroundings.

Darcy's eyes followed him as he turned a corner in the path, then disappeared. *He'll be safe now*, she thought. She was glad that they'd all decided not to take any chances yesterday. The woods seemed much quieter today.

Just then an explosion ripped through the air.

Gunfire!

Panic hit the girls as they sprang into action. They barreled down the path, their legs pumping beneath them.

Darcy rushed ahead, nearly sliding into the bushes at the curve of the path. That was when she saw him spread out in the snow.

Claw had been shot!

"Oh my gosh!" Darcy whispered, rushing over to his motionless body. "Claw . . . can you hear me?"

There was no answer.

"He's unconscious," Francie said, looking around warily. "And the hunters will be here any second. We've got to hide him."

Darcy and Francie each grabbed one furry leg and tugged. With a lot of effort, they managed to drag Claw under the cover of a snowy evergreen. But as soon as Darcy climbed back out, she saw the tracks they'd left. The hunters would figure things out. Already she could hear the buzz of their snowmobiles.

"We've got to cover these tracks," she said.

Fiona's dark eyes lit on an idea, and she plunged backward over the trail. "Snow angels!" she said, fanning her arms and legs through the snow. "Help me."

"You guys go ahead," said Francie. "I'm going back to the house to get the sled. And I've got to create some kind of distraction."

Darcy looked up from where she was scooping snow into a mound over Claw's prints. "What are you going to do?"

"I don't know," Francie said. "But we've got to get the hunters out of this area before they search it. I'll think of something along the way," she called as she disappeared down the path.

When the hunters arrived a minute later, Darcy and Fiona were pretending to be in the middle of a snowball fight. The tracks were now a trampled mess of footprints and snow angels.

"Girls?" Mr. Black seemed concerned as he swung his leg over the snowmobile. "Didn't the sheriff warn you about these woods?"

"Yes, sir," Darcy said, rolling a snowball in her mitten. "But I live just over the hill. We didn't think it would be dangerous if we stayed close to home."

The other hunters shook their heads and muttered to one another.

"Did you hear that shot?" one man asked.

Darcy nodded.

"It scared the stuffing out of me," Fiona answered. "Did you think *I* was the Claw? Did you shoot at me because I'm wearing white snow pants?"

"No!" A hunter with a red jacket stepped forward. "I fired that shot. I had the beast in my sight. It's got to be around here somewhere," he said, poking his rifle into a snowy bush.

"If it was around here, we would have seen it," Darcy said.

"Maybe you made a mistake," Mr. Black told the hunter. "The girl *is* wearing white, and—"

"I'd *never* shoot at a kid," the hunter with the red jacket insisted. "Never. I saw the bear." He hitched his rifle over his shoulder, adding, "And I hit my mark."

It's true! Darcy wanted to shout, biting her lip. She hoped Claw was okay, but she couldn't stop thinking about his lifeless form under the tree.

Just then one of the hunters' radios crackled, and a man near the snowmobiles tuned it in. "Sheriff's office says there's been another sighting," he announced. "Someone saw the Claw over by the Bitter Cliffs."

Quickly, the men mounted the snowmobiles.

"You girls should head home," Mr. Black told them. "You're better off playing in sight of the ranch, Darcy."

She nodded as the engines revved and the vehicles sped off.

Fiona stood by the evergreen, her hands folded in front of her as she whispered, "Can we check on him?"

"We'd better wait," Darcy answered. That hunter had been so annoyed, she wouldn't put it past him to spy on them.

"Hey," Francie called breathlessly from the path. She was tugging the sled, covered with snow gear and the blanket. "Sorry I took so long. I ran back to the ranch to make the call." She looked around, then asked, "Did they head off to the Cliffs?"

"How did you know that?" Fiona asked. "Someone spotted a bear there."

"You made that call?" Darcy asked. When Francie nodded, she added, "Good thinking. It sent them buzzing out of here before they had a chance to snoop around."

While Fiona stood watch, Darcy and Francie pulled the sled right under the evergreen. Claw was stretched out there, still as a stone.

The two girls knelt beside him. Darcy took his paw while Francie leaned over him.

"There's no blood," she said, examining his chest. "The hunter must have fired this dart." She pulled the shiny object from his chest. It reminded Darcy of a skinny pen.

"Maybe it was filled with a sedative," Darcy said hopefully.

"Or a poison," Francie added grimly. She

moved behind him and lifted his head. "Either way, we've got to get him to a safe place. Help me lift him onto the sled."

🦇 🦇 🦇

The trip back to the Mackies' house seemed to take forever. The girls couldn't stop worrying about Claw, so silent and still under the Mackies' plaid blanket.

They passed a few kids, some dragging their sleds to Winslow Hill. Another group was making a snowman. But they moved quickly, afraid that someone would ask about the bundle on the sled.

At last, Darcy tugged the sled into the Mackies' backyard. They'd made it.

"Girls?" came a familiar voice.

Darcy froze.

The back door popped open and Lila Mackie emerged, hugging herself in the cold. "Thank goodness you're okay. Sheriff Smoke just called. Were you playing in the woods, Fiona?"

"Ye-e-es," Fiona answered timidly.

"After all the warnings about that bear?" Fiona's mother marched across the yard, frowning at the girls.

"And you two should know better," she told Francie and Darcy.

"I'm sorry, Aunt Lila," Darcy said, nervously tugging her braids under her chin. "We were close to the ranch, and we—"

"That's no reason to take any chances," Lila said, shivering.

"Are you mad?" Fiona asked.

"I'm mad because I care about what happens to you," her mother said. "All of you. You must be cold as icicles. I'll make some hot chocolate if you . . ."

Her voice trailed off as her eyes lit on the sled.

Uh-oh! Darcy thought, biting her lower lip.

"Fiona?" Lila said sternly. "Is that my new blanket?" She reached down, grabbed the corner of the blue plaid blanket . . .

And lifted it off the sled!

13

"This is not a toy," Mrs. Mackie went on, waving the blanket in the air.

Meanwhile, Darcy nervously eyed the sled.

Claw was wrapped up in two burlap bundles marked OATS. Francie had picked them up in the barn after she'd called the sheriff. "We can't pass Claw off as a dog forever," she'd explained.

Darcy just hoped that they could pass him off as two sacks of oats.

"Sorry, Mom," Fiona said. "We were building a tent in the shed. And then we used the blanket to cover the sled. And then, I forgot to bring it back."

"You need to be more responsible," Fiona's mother told her.

"I'm only six," Fiona muttered.

"Old enough to know better," Mrs. Mackie replied. She folded the blanket under one arm and noticed the sled. "Oats?"

"We're delivering them," Darcy said quickly. "To the Petersons. They're buying a horse."

"Really?" Lila blinked. "I heard they just got an enormous dog." She turned toward the house, calling back, "I'll put the cocoa on."

"Thanks," the girls called after her.

"That was close," Fiona said under her breath. "I thought I was going to get ground up."

"You mean *grounded*," Darcy said. "We're just lucky your mom is so nice."

Francie was already dragging the sled toward the aluminum shed. "Open the door, will ya?"

Fiona tugged open the door, and the other girls maneuvered the sled inside. It was warmer in the shed, which made Darcy feel a little better. But her spirits sank when she pulled the burlap sack off Claw's head. He was still unconscious.

Darcy pressed her head against his chest. "I can hear a heartbeat . . . but it's very slow."

"And his breathing is shallow," Francie added, her pretty face strained with worry.

"Is he ever going to wake up?" Fiona asked.

"I wish I knew." Francie held up the dart that had hit him in the chest. "Seems to me, if this was filled with a tranquilizer, he'd be waking up by now."

"What do you mean?" Fiona's freckled nose scrunched up. "What else could be in the dart?"

Francie gave Darcy a solemn look. "It might have been filled with poison."

"Poison!" Fiona let out a whimper. "We have to do something," she said, stroking Claw's arm. "We can't let him die."

"I know, Fee," Darcy said softly, "but we're not doctors. The best we can do right now is keep him safe and warm."

"No!" Fiona squeaked. She tugged off one mitten and swiped at a tear that was rolling down her cheek. "We can't just sit around."

Francie slumped down on an overturned crate and sighed. "It's so frustrating. If I were still a fairy, I could make everything better. I could heal Claw and get him back to Monsterville in the blink of an eye."

So she still thinks about being a fairy, Darcy thought. *It must be great, having magic powers. Wiping mounds of snow away. Fixing broken bike chains . . .* Instead, Francie had chosen to be a girl, with no special powers at all.

"It must be hard to give up your magic powers," Darcy said, touching Francie's shoulder. "But I like you the way you are."

"Me, too," Fiona agreed. "Even if you're only a girl."

"A smart girl," Darcy added. "We've got to think hard. There's got to be something we can do for Claw, even if we *don't* have pixie dust in our fingertips."

"Maybe Claw is just hibernating," Fiona said hopefully. "Maybe the cold has finally gotten to him."

"Bears don't hibernate," Darcy said. "Most winters they go into a deep sleep. They can sleep with their eyes open. But their breathing and heartbeat don't slow down."

"Besides," Francie pointed out, "Claw has been all over the Arctic. Why would the cold bother him now?"

"We need a doctor," Fiona said firmly. "But if we call an ambulance, everyone will know about Claw."

"That would be disastrous," Francie said. "They'll stick him in a research lab. Or even worse, a zoo."

"What we really need is a veterinarian," Darcy said, thinking of the animal doctor who'd been to the ranch a few times over the years. "But we can't let Dr. Frankel come here."

"That's for sure," Fiona said. "My mom is already mad at us."

"Let's visit Dr. Frankel's office," Darcy suggested. "Maybe if we just describe the symptoms, he can give us an antidote."

"And when he asks about the patient?" Francie prodded. "What are we going to tell him?"

"I'll think of something," Darcy said, pulling on her mittens.

🦇 🦇 🦇

Fiona's head barely reached the high table in Dr. Frankel's examining room. She peered up at him hopefully as Darcy fished in her pocket for the rifle cartridge. Francie had stayed behind to take care of Claw.

"So," the doctor said, scribbling some notes on a clipboard. His gray hair had always reminded Darcy of a lion's mane. And sometimes, when Dr. Frankel spoke, his voice came out like a roar. "My assistant says we have a dire emergency here," he growled. "Where's the patient?"

"He couldn't make it," Fiona said. "He's at home, sleeping."

"Really?" he said sternly, peering down at Fiona. "And who are you?"

"Fiona Mackie," she said.

"My cousin," Darcy explained. She held the dart out to Dr. Frankel. "This is what hit him . . . I mean, the animal."

He took the cartridge and examined it carefully. "And what kind of animal did you say this was?"

"Well," Darcy said haltingly, "it's, um . . . bigger than a dog. But smaller than a horse."

"And it likes carrot sticks and snow," Fiona added.

The doctor scowled at them. "What is this, twenty questions?"

The girls clammed up.

"Tell me what happened," he demanded. "What was hit by this dart?"

"It's a secret," Fiona said. "Is the dart filled with poison?"

"That depends on what it hit," he said impatiently. He put the clipboard and dart on the table and folded his arms. "Now I know you're trying to cover something up. And I don't appreciate games, girls."

"We're not playing," Fiona said, her chin trembling.

"Are you trying to treat a wild creature?" he asked, his voice nearly a whisper.

Darcy squirmed and stared at the ground. So much for avoiding the truth.

Beside her, Fiona shuffled her feet restlessly.

Dr. Frankel lifted Darcy's chin so that she was forced to look him in the eyes. "If there was a sick animal at your ranch, your mother would have called me to come out there," he said.

Silence.

Darcy couldn't argue with that. She knew it was true.

She had to think of something . . . fast.

14

"Go on, Darcy," Fiona suddenly said. "Tell him the truth."

What? Darcy wanted to glare at her cousin, but she couldn't take her eyes away from the scowling vet.

"The truth . . ." Her throat was so dry that the words came out in a squeak. "The truth is that, my mom doesn't know about this," she began. At least that part was true.

"Mmm-hmm," he murmured. "And?"

"And, well, I know all about wild animals. That they're dangerous and everything," Darcy went on. "But the animal that was hit isn't wild." Well, that part was true, too.

"Then why didn't your mother call me?" the vet probed.

"Because she doesn't know," Darcy blabbered on. "We weren't supposed to take the horses outside the corral. But Gingersnap needed exercise, and I guess one of the hunters thought she was a deer or something, 'cause—"

"Gingersnap?" Fiona's nose wrinkled in confusion.

Darcy shot her a warning glance, and Fiona covered her mouth, as if to keep from letting anything else slip out.

"So the colt was hit . . ." Dr. Frankel said under his breath.

The lie burned deep inside Darcy, but she couldn't think of any other way to help Claw.

She nodded. "She's asleep now. And her heartbeat is really slow." She glanced over at the dart. "Is she going to make it?"

The veterinarian rubbed his chin. "This cartridge is filled with a powerful sedative. It's a high dosage for a colt."

"Is there anything we can do?" Fiona asked.

The doctor sucked in his breath, as if he were getting ready to blow up. Darcy frowned. Dr. Frankel loved animals. But he didn't have a lot of patience for kids.

But to Darcy's surprise, he didn't lecture them. Instead he went to a white cabinet against the wall and opened a glass door. He took out a small bottle with an eyedropper on top.

"I must be nuts. But I won't let an animal suffer because you're afraid to fess up to your mother."

He handed her the bottle. "Take this and give the horse two droppers-full every hour until it comes to. Got that? Two droppers-full each hour."

"Yes, sir," Darcy said, relief flooding through her.

"And next time, obey your mother."

"Yes, sir," Darcy said, smiling. "Thank you, Dr. Frankel."

"Yeah! Thanks, Doc!" Fiona added, grabbing Darcy's arm. They scooted out of the office, eager to get away before he could change his mind.

Ten minutes later, they were back at the Mackies', winded but excited.

"This should help," Darcy said, holding out the bottle. She explained the dosage to Francie, who filled the dropper and squeezed it into Claw's mouth. Then she repeated the process.

"What do we do now?" Fiona asked, petting Claw's head.

"Watch . . . and wait," Francie answered solemnly.

The minutes dragged on.

Darcy reminded herself that they'd done everything they could. She'd even lied to Dr. Frankel. She thought of Dee and Gee and the other yetis. They hadn't seen their father for five years! The medicine was going to work. It *had* to.

Much more confident, Fiona went into the house and brought back an armful of stuffed animals. "So Claw has someone to keep him company when he wakes up," she said.

If he wakes up, Darcy thought somberly.

By the time five o'clock rolled around, she couldn't wait any longer. "We have to get home for dinner," she reminded Francie. It was already getting dark outside.

"Okay." Reluctantly, Francie wrapped her scarf around her neck. "Call us as soon as he wakes up," she told Fiona. She brushed the fur back from Claw's brow and whispered, "Bye, Claw."

The girls were at the door when the words rasped out, "Bye, Francie."

Darcy and Francie whirled around in surprise.

Fiona's hands were in the air. "I didn't say it!"

They rushed to Claw's side, and he popped one shiny eye open. "What's with the long faces?" he asked.

"You were shot!" Fiona said. "You were shot. And there was a big fat dart in your chest. And I was afraid you were going to die. But the vet gave us some medicine for you, even though Darcy told him you were a horse."

"Is that right?" He sat up and rubbed his eyes. "Sounds like I missed all the excitement."

"You *are* the excitement," Francie said, squeezing his arm.

Darcy's heart leaped in her chest. She'd been

wondering if she'd ever see Claw awake again. "Welcome back," she said.

"Thanks," he said, closing his eyes for a second. "My head feels like it's stuffed with cotton, but I'm glad to be here. Those hunters would have made mincemeat out of me."

"Gross," Fiona squeaked. "I hate mincemeat. But I like pumpkin pie." She grinned. "I brought you a friend." She handed him her blue teddy bear.

"That's awfully nice of you," he said quietly. "If I didn't have a family waiting, I'd never leave this little shed."

"I wish you could stay," Fiona said.

"But we'll get you back to Monsterville," Francie said.

"Tomorrow afternoon," Darcy added. "And that's a promise."

🦇 🦇 🦇

"Good morning, sunshine!" Francie said, beaming a smile from the doorway of Darcy's bedroom.

Darcy yawned and looked at the clock. "Nine-thirty?" She bolted up in bed. "We overslept."

"Not when there's no school," Francie said. She went to the window and pulled up the shade. Outside, the world sparkled. The trees and hills were buried in a thick blanket of snow.

"It must have snowed all night," Darcy said as Francie sat on the edge of the bed.

"So much that school is canceled. The pass on Highway 93 has been closed." She leaned closer to Darcy to add, "And we have the whole day to get Claw back to Monsterville."

Darcy snapped her fingers. "That's great! We can strap on our snowshoes and head up the trail."

After a quick breakfast of oatmeal loaded with walnuts, bananas, and raisins, the girls pulled on their snow gear and headed outside to have a look.

Expecting to see miles of untouched snow, Darcy frowned at all the tracks on the hill. "That's strange." She squinted into the sun and spotted half a dozen people bobbing along the trail at the edge of the woods. Sheriff Smoke's Jeep was parked on the access road. And from the distant buzz, she could tell that snowmobilers were already running the trails.

The area was teeming with people!

"It's like a big picnic," she said aloud. "Just because we have a day off from school?"

"I don't know," Francie said. "But I didn't expect the woods to be so busy today."

They were headed up the hill when someone called Darcy's name. She turned and spotted Annabel Mackinac trudging through the snow.

Torie trailed behind her, the video camera slung over her shoulder.

"We heard about yesterday," Annabel said. "How you almost ran into the Claw again." She turned to Torie and snapped, "Get the camera going, idiot."

"All right, already." With an annoyed look, Torie hoisted the camera and pointed it at Darcy.

"Now," Annabel said. "Is it true that the Claw came after you again? That he scratched your cousin because she was wearing white snow pants?"

"That's not true at all," Darcy protested, pushing the camera out of her face. "It's a bunch of lies."

"Let's get out of here," Francie muttered, trudging ahead.

"Wait!" Annabel called after them. "What about that hunter who saw the beast? Is *he* lying?"

But Darcy refused to turn around. She was plodding up the hill when something cold and hard hit her head.

"Ouch!" Touching her neck, she found crumbs of snow in her hair. She spun around.

Annabel had pelted her with a snowball!

The girl stood back with her arms folded, a smug expression on her face.

"You little . . ." Steaming mad, Darcy made a move toward the girl, but Francie held her back with a gentle hand on her arm.

"Let her go," Francie said quietly. "I want to talk with Sheriff Smoke before he heads out."

Ahead, Darcy saw a group of hunters wave to the sheriff as they sped off on their snowmobiles. *Francie is right,* she thought, clenching her hands into fists. But she'd love the chance to wing a snowball—right into Annabel's smug little face!

Sheriff Smoke nodded at Darcy and Francie. "I know *you* don't have to be told twice to stay away from here," he said. "But people seem to think this wild bear is some sort of joke. It's going to take me all morning to clear the nosy people away from here."

Darcy's heart sank down to her toes.

There was no way they could sneak Claw past this circus. They'd have to call off the trip to Monsterville!

"It's no use," Darcy said as she hung her hat on a hook in the mudroom. "We can't take Claw through those woods today."

"I'll call Fiona and tell her to keep him in the shed," Francie said. She tugged off her boots. "Poor Claw. He's going to be so disappointed."

"Maybe we can take him tomorrow," Darcy suggested.

"I don't know," Francie said as she went to the window in her stockinged feet. "Not with half the world thinking they're going to catch a look at a big beast. I'm beginning to think this excitement is here to stay."

While Francie called the Mackies, Darcy pulled on an old sweatshirt that came down to her knees. She brought a hairbrush into the living room and plopped down on the sofa. Her hair was still wet from the snowball, and it was more tangled than usual since she hadn't taken the time to braid it that morning.

Francie came in, decked out in a pink sweat suit and her fuzzy bear slippers. She shuffled over to the sofa. "Fiona is holding down the fort," she said, taking the brush and working on Darcy's hair.

"I can just imagine," Darcy said. "I'm surprised that she didn't bring Claw in to have breakfast with the family."

"No," Francie said. "But she did smuggle out some huckleberry pancakes."

"I hope she was careful," Darcy said. "If Aunt Lila gets a look at Claw, we're dead meat."

"She promised to play it cool," Francie said.

Darcy sighed. It felt good to be warm, snuggled on the couch. The stroke of the hairbrush was soothing. The only problem was, she couldn't help feeling terrible for Claw. Another day he wouldn't see his family.

It wasn't fair.

"I feel bad," she told Francie. "I'm beginning to wonder if Claw will *ever* get home."

"Hmm." Francie brushed Darcy's hair into a ponytail and paused. "The woods are impassable."

"That's for sure," Darcy said.

"But if people want the Claw," Francie added thoughtfully, "maybe we should deliver."

"What?" Darcy flashed her a confused look, but

Francie's gaze was fixed on her bear slippers.

"You know the old saying—Give the people what they want? Maybe we can use the Claw to lure the crowd away from the woods." Francie's green eyes were lit with excitement. "What if we make it look like the Claw has been in town?"

"I don't know." Darcy hesitated. "It's too dangerous to bring Claw to the center of town."

"But that's the glory of it!" Francie added, clapping her hands together. "He doesn't need to be there at all." When Darcy shook her head, Francie jumped up from the sofa and motioned toward the mudroom. "Gear up, sister. We're going to create a stir that'll attract everyone in Whiterock."

Kids packed the booths of the Dairy Saloon. Darcy recognized Stacy Redcloud slurping whipped cream from a cup of cocoa. At another booth, a bunch of boys were using french fries as torpedoes.

"It's pretty crowded," she told Francie, who stood behind her with a shopping bag under one arm. "I guess they're celebrating the day off."

"Perfect," Francie said, looking over her shoulder. "But we'd better start out back, so nobody sees us setting up."

Behind the Dairy Saloon was a patio with

picnic tables. Kids usually took their ice cream outside in the summer, but now everything was covered with a blanket of snow.

Making sure no one was watching, Francie
reached into the shopping bag. She pulled out her
bear slippers. She'd done a little work on them
before she and Darcy left the house. Using Popsicle
sticks and Krazy Glue, the girls had added extra
long claws to the bear toes.

"This should make a great print," Francie said,
slipping out of her boots. "I'll do the Claw tracks.
You do the message."

"Gotcha!" Darcy said, reaching into the bag.
Before the first snowfall, she and Francie had col-
lected some fallen pine branches and cones to use
for a school project. Darcy had never imagined
how handy they'd be.

Where was the best spot for the message? She
eyed the area carefully. The picnic tables were too
flat. And it might not be seen on the ground.

Then she spotted a storm door leading to the
basement of the Dairy Saloon. The door was covered
with snow—and had just the right amount of tilt.

Carefully, she pressed the first pinecone into
the bed of snow. Then she used two bent pine
branches to make the rest of the *B*.

She stood back and squinted. The letter was
clear. This was going to work.

Meanwhile Francie was using the slippers to make bear tracks. She tromped to the wooded area at the edge of the patio, then doubled back.

"This is fun," she said, pressing her foot into the fresh snow. When she stepped away, the imprint of a footpad with five clawed toes was visible in the snow.

Within minutes, the girls were finished. Francie had left Claw prints all over the area. She'd even climbed over the top of one of the picnic tables!

And Darcy had left the legendary message— BEWARE THE CLAW—spelled out on the storm door.

"Now we just have to get someone to notice it," Darcy said as Francie stepped back into her boots.

Lifting her soggy slippers, she wrinkled her nose. "These may never be the same again." With a sigh, she shoved them back into the shopping bag. "Let's go inside. I'll buy you a hot chocolate."

"Wait," Darcy said, following Francie around the corner of the building. "What if no one notices this stuff? Kids aren't going to go around back to the patio in the snow."

"I'll take care of it," Francie said with a smile.

The door jingled as the girls stepped into the ice cream shop. They pressed past a couple of kids ordering burgers to go and climbed onto counter stools.

"Two hot chocolates," Darcy told the guy

behind the counter. "With extra whipped cream."

Francie winked at Darcy, then said in a loud voice. "Can you *believe* that Annabel?"

"You mean the snowball attack?" Darcy asked under her breath.

"The videotape that's going to be on 'Outrageous Videos,'" Francie announced.

The kids in the take-out line shot a look at Francie.

Darcy blinked. *What the heck was Francie talking about?*

"She's going to send it off this afternoon," Francie went on. She was talking so loud that lots of kids were staring now. "I just saw her setting up her camera outside, on the patio."

The patio! Darcy was beginning to get the idea.

"Annabel wants to get a few more people on tape," Francie said, casting a sidelong glance at some girls in a booth. "You know, local reaction."

"Really?" Darcy said, faking interest. "Maybe we should go out. I'd *love* to be in her video."

Before the last words were out of Darcy's mouth, the girls were sliding out of their booth. Darcy saw Stacy's black hair swaying behind her as she rushed out the door.

She bit back a smile as she turned to Francie. Would their plan work?

Francie paid for the cocoa. The girls were

heading out the door, cups in hand, when a raw shriek split the air.

Gripping her hot cup, Darcy poked her head around the side of the building and saw the four girls clustered around the storm door.

"The Claw!" Stacy screamed.

The door to the saloon jingled as kids piled out, rushing to the source of the excitement.

"Whoa! Tracks!" one kid shouted.

"Better call the sheriff," someone said. "He'll want to set up a crime scene or something."

Darcy moved back to the front of the building and smiled.

"Yes!" Francie said, raising her mitten to slap her a high five.

The girls were pleased by the initial reaction to the "Claw" scene. But they weren't sure it was enough to do the trick. Would the hunters and newshounds like Annabel go for it?

Darcy and Francie decided to head home and find out. They were just a few blocks from the Dairy Saloon when they spotted the flashing lights of Sheriff Smoke's Jeep. The vehicle roared past them, heading toward the saloon.

"It's a start," Darcy said hopefully.

By the time they got back to the ranch, they'd passed more than a dozen snowmobiles heading into town. And the woods at the top of the hill seemed deserted.

"Looking good," Francie said as they headed up to check out the trail.

The trampled path was the only sign of the crowds that had tromped through there that morning. The forest was quiet.

"No sound of snowmobiles," Francie said.

"Or snoopy girls," Darcy added. "I hope Annabel's tape freezes up in her camera."

Francie nodded toward the ranch. "Let's call Fiona and get our buddy on the road."

When Darcy dialed the Mackies' number, Sam answered the phone.

"So . . . it's my sneaky cousin," he said in a muffled voice. "Just how long do you think you can slip a big bear past me?"

"You *saw* him?" Darcy said, her stomach churning. "Oh, Sam. Don't tell me your parents found out about Claw!"

"Almost," he answered. "Fiona is the worst at keeping secrets. Mom and Dad would have run right into him if I hadn't distracted them. I *knew* something was going on. Why didn't you tell me?"

"You were busy," Darcy said, wrapping the phone cord around her finger. "At least, you were the first day we met him. And then, well, I know you're scared of animals—"

"Just dogs," he interrupted. "And I'm not scared. I'm allergic."

"Well, we kept thinking that we were going to send him back to Monsterville, but things just got in our way."

"No kidding," Sam answered. "I think everyone

in town is out looking for Claw now. Even Mom and Dad. Did you hear that there's been a sighting at the Dairy Saloon?"

"Oh, I heard," Darcy said with a laugh. "That was part one of our plan. Now, here's part two. . . ."

* * *

"They should be here soon," Darcy told Francie when she hung up the phone. She sat down at the kitchen table and poured herself a glass of milk. "They're bringing the sled. And they're going to hide Claw in the burlap sacks again."

"They?" Francie repeated.

Darcy nodded. "Sam found out. It's a good thing. Fiona almost spilled the beans to the whole neighborhood."

Francie laughed as she spread peanut butter onto a cracker. "Telegram. Telephone. Tell-a-Fiona."

"She still can't keep a secret," Darcy agreed. "I'm just glad we've got a shot at getting Claw home today. Your plan to get everyone out of the woods was great!" Darcy wanted to mention the thing that had been bothering her the last day or so—the worry that Francie still missed being a fairy. She couldn't come right out and say it. But maybe she could make her point another way. "And you pulled it all off without any fairy dust at all."

"Thanks," Francie said, handing Darcy a

cracker glopped with peanut butter. "Being a girl is a lot harder than I ever expected. Everything's twice as hard when you don't have magic in your fingertips."

"But you do." Darcy put the cracker down and picked up Francie's hand. "These hands do magical things every day. Here at the house. With the animals. At school . . ."

"Just the normal things that normal girls do," Francie said. "That's why I feel guilty about giving up on all my good deeds."

"*Guilty?*" Darcy couldn't believe what she was hearing. "Francie, even if you're not a fairy anymore, you never stopped sharing your magic. You do good deeds every day. I can't count the times you've helped me out of trouble."

"That doesn't count." Francie waved her away. "You're like a sister to me. It's easy to help out people you like."

"But you always go one step further," Darcy insisted. "You help out my mom all the time. You're so patient with Fiona. All the kids at the middle school think you're great. And you've got something that most fairies don't seem to have."

Francie blinked as Darcy pointed to her head and said: "Brain power. You're the one who came up with the clever ideas to get Claw out of this mess. Calling in the sighting at the Cliffs to get the hunters off our backs. Hiding him in the burlap sacks. Even the diversion at the Dairy Saloon."

"I was just trying to help," Francie said.

"Exactly. Have you ever thought that maybe you can do more good in the world as a girl?"

"I never saw it that way," Francie said, her green eyes sparkling with a new light. "I guess I shouldn't feel so guilty about living my life the way I want—as a girl."

Darcy washed down a cracker with a swallow of milk. She took a deep breath. "So you're planning to stick around?" she asked timidly. "I mean, you *don't* want to go back to being a fairy?"

"And give up my new cousins and sister?" Francie jumped out of her chair and gave Darcy an impulsive hug. "Absolutely not!"

"There they are," Darcy said, pointing downhill. After a quick lunch, the girls had bundled up in their snow gear and climbed to the edge of the woods to wait.

The lumpy sled dragged behind Sam, who moved at a steady pace. Fiona toddled along behind him, trying to catch snowflakes on her tongue.

The snow had started at noon, and from the white sky, Darcy didn't think it was going to stop anytime soon.

"Hey," Sam called ahead. "Great day for a sleigh ride."

"Especially since we have the woods to ourselves," Francie called back. She and Darcy had checked the trail and found it deserted. It seemed that everyone in Whiterock had rushed to the Dairy Saloon for a look at the Claw prints.

When Sam reached the top of the hill, Darcy

107

helped him tug the sled into the woods, behind the cover of some snow-covered boulders.

"Wow," Darcy said, staring down at the bundles on the sled. "You really made him look like two sacks of oats."

"When I do a job, I don't mess around," Sam said.

Claw poked his head out of one sack and smiled. "We needed a little extra stuffing," he said, pulling out the blue plaid blanket.

"I told him Mom is gonna kill us," Fiona said, wrapping the blanket over her shoulders. "But Sam wouldn't listen."

"At last," Claw said. He sprang off the sled and sniffed the air. "No scent of humans here—besides you," he told the kids. "I'm going to make it home today. I can feel it in my bones."

He still wore a bandage on his shoulder, but Claw towered above them with grace and strength. Darcy was glad to see him looking healthy.

"We're going to Monsterville," Fiona chanted. "We're going to Monsterville!"

"We are?" Sam blinked. When it came to the town of ghouls, Sam was reluctant to pay another visit so soon.

"We promised Claw that we'd show him the way," Darcy explained.

"Besides," Francie said, "after what happened yesterday, I won't rest easy until I see the big guy step out of these woods. You should've seen the packs of hunters around here, Sam."

"I know, I know," he said. "I got an earful from Fiona." He tucked the sled behind the boulders and zipped his jacket up to his chin. Darcy was relieved to see he wasn't going to argue about their plan. "What are we waiting for?" Sam asked. "Let's hit the trail!"

An hour later, Darcy's feet were beginning to feel like lead weights. Snow was flying everywhere, and every step demanded a lot of energy.

"I'm snow-blind," Fiona said, batting at the falling flakes. She was riding on Claw's shoulders. Her little legs had given out soon after they'd passed the wooden bridge.

"At least you've got a ride," Darcy told her. She didn't want to complain, but she wasn't sure how much further she could go.

"Maybe we should take a break," Francie said. She was struggling through a snowdrift that came up to her waist. There was no way around it. Mounds of snow had formed right on the trail, blocking the way.

"Maybe we should rethink our plan," Sam said, pulling Francie toward him.

Darcy cupped one hand over her eyes and

looked around her. From what she could see of the trail, they were barely halfway to Monsterville. Barely halfway! And they'd been plodding through snow for an hour.

"I hate to say it, guys," Francie said through chattering teeth. "But maybe we should turn back. This snow is a real pain in the neck."

Through the flurries, Darcy could see the grim look on Sam's face. "It's just too heavy," he said. "We're going to wear ourselves out if we keep moving."

"I wish I could help," Claw said, glancing down at them. "I would carry all of you, if I could."

"I know," Francie said, patting his arm. "But you're just one yeti."

"We'd better find a place to hole up," Sam said. "We have to stay put until this storm blows over."

"How long will that be?" Fiona asked.

The question hung in the cold, snowy air.

"We'll see, Fee," Darcy said quietly. The scary part was, there was no telling how long it might be. Still, Darcy knew that Sam had the right idea. It was another lesson her mother had drilled into her head: *In a heavy snowstorm, if you can't get home, the thing to do is find shelter and stay put.*

"We need to find a sheltered area," Sam said.

The kids looked around. It was hard to see through the curtain of white. Darcy could make out some tall trees in the distance, but there wasn't much cover underneath them. Otherwise, they were surrounded by brambles.

"Over there," Claw said, pointing off the path. "There are some cliffs. We might be able to find a cave."

"Probably Bitter Cliffs," Francie said, squinting into the snow.

"Let's give it a try," Sam said. He linked his arm with Francie's.

Claw took Darcy's hand and helped her climb over the snow-covered vines. It was rough going, but soon they came to the cliffs. Claw lowered Fiona to the snow. "I'll check the area," he said. "Wouldn't want to meet up with a den of bears."

The kids waited, shivering, as he searched the rocky hillside. A few minutes later, he returned and led them away.

"No caves nearby," he said. "But I did find a ledge that's protected from the snow. We can warm up in there."

The kids followed the yeti to the gray slab of rock, two feet above the ground. Sam helped Francie and Darcy up while Claw hoisted Fiona into place. He had to duck under the rock overhang, but the ledge went back far enough to get out of the wind and snow.

"This would be a great fort," Fiona said.

"Thanks for finding it," Francie told Claw. "We'll be okay here. You'd better go on ahead."

"Absolutely," Sam agreed. "You don't want to be here when the snow stops, Claw. There'll be hunters, maybe even the sheriff."

"I won't leave you," Claw said.

"But you have to," Darcy insisted. "The snow doesn't hold you back at all. It's your element. You'll be in Monsterville in no time."

"I won't go," Claw said firmly. He settled back against the wall of the ledge and motioned the kids to come closer. Fiona plopped onto his lap. Then Claw reached forward and enveloped the kids in his furry arms. His body gave off a glow that warmed through Darcy's jacket.

"That's better," Fiona said, sighing. She leaned her head back against the white fur and closed her eyes.

"At least we won't freeze," Sam admitted.

Huddled against Claw's warm chest, Darcy knew they'd be safe for a while.

"We were really stupid to head out without any food or supplies," Francie said quietly.

"And the sky was so white," Darcy admitted. "I thought we might be in for another storm."

"Think positive," Sam said. "We're together. And we've got Claw to keep us warm. That's pretty lucky. We'll be okay here for a while."

The kids nodded silently. The only sound was the howling wind.

No one wanted to say the awful truth.

They were trapped—snowbound. And there was no way of knowing if they would ever get out of this mess.

"... That was when I sent Marta down to Monsterville. I was supposed to join her the next month, but my timing was off," Claw explained.

He had been telling the kids stories of his travels in the Arctic, and his deep, gritty voice was lulling Darcy to sleep.

How long have we been sitting here? Darcy wondered. *Minutes? Hours?* Claw was keeping them warm enough, but there wasn't much he could do about Darcy's growling stomach. She wished she'd eaten a few extra peanut butter crackers at lunch.

"Just as I was about to head south," Claw continued, "the ice started melting. The ice caps were breaking around us, making travel impossible. We had to get to high ground."

"What did you do?" Fiona asked.

"I didn't want to wait another year to see my family. So I tried to swim between the ice floes. Let me tell you, that water is cold. But the problem is the moving ice. If you get trapped between . . ."

Darcy's mind trailed off. Claw had been through so much. And now, when he was finally almost home, he was stuck with a bunch of kids who were too stupid to bring their skis.

She was falling into a funk when she heard those funny noises. . . .

Pop!

Boink!

Ping!

She pushed out of Claw's arms and peered into the falling snow. Could it be . . . ?

Her heart lifted at the sight of the blinking lights—purple, blue, and orange.

The fairy squadron was hovering outside!

"Hoshi! Neona!" she called through the opening. "We're in here!"

"I knew you were around here somewhere," Hoshi cried as she zipped past Darcy's face. "What the heck are you doing in here?"

"At least it's dry!" Beryl sputtered into the covered area and shook out her wings. "My cold is coming back. I can feel it."

"Guys!" Francie's face was lit with wonder. "What are you doing here?"

"We knew you were in trouble!" Hoshi exclaimed. "We fairies have a sixth sense about things like that."

"But I thought you had trouble flying in a snowstorm," Darcy said.

"Boy, do we!" Neona agreed, glowing orange. "For a minute there, I was sure we took a wrong turn toward the North Pole."

"You could've visited Santa," Fiona crowed.

"But we had to find you," Beryl said.

"We can't stand to let a good deed go undone," Hoshi added with a burst of purple. "Especially when someone needs help."

"It was really nice of you to come," Francie said, flashing the pixies a grateful smile.

"Definitely," Sam said. "So, can you build us a snowmobile? Or better yet, make the snow stop?"

"We can't control the weather," Beryl admitted.

"But we *can* work around it," Hoshi said. "Somehow, we're going to get you to Monsterville."

"How?" Fiona asked the question that was on everyone's mind.

"Let's see," Hoshi said, fluttering. "We're going to have to pool our magic."

"Definitely," Neona said. "Time for a fairy ring."

"What's that?" Fiona asked.

"Shh." Francie took her by the hand. "Let them concentrate."

The three fairies were already flying in a circle. They hovered for a moment, then joined hands and started spinning.

Fiona grinned. "It's just like ring around the—"

"Shh!" Darcy whispered, afraid that her cousin would interrupt the magic.

The fairies spun around, forming rings of purple, orange, and blue. As they moved faster, their colors began to form a band of white light. They were chirping, too. At least, that's what Darcy thought. But when she listened carefully, she began to make out words. They were chanting:

"TWINKLING, SPARKLING FAIRY DUST,
CARRY US THROUGH THE STORM.
TO MONSTERVILLE WE GO, WE MUST,
AND KEEP US SAFE AND WARM!"

Darcy watched in awe as they repeated the chant, spinning wildly. White sparks were flying from the fairy ring. Suddenly, with a burst of light, the ring exploded. . . .

And white sparks rained down on the ledge.

Darcy gasped as the tiny sparkles fizzled onto her head and shoulders. It was like being showered by fireworks, only the sparks weren't hot at all. They tickled!

"Jump back, Jack!" Hoshi exclaimed, rubbing her eyes. The explosion had knocked the three fairies onto the rock floor.

"That was some piece of magic," Beryl said,

rubbing her tiny rear end. "Did it work?"

It had left everyone speechless—even Fiona, who gazed in awe with eyes as wide as saucers.

"Maybe there's a snowmobile waiting outside," Sam said, peering out through the opening. "Nope. No such luck."

"Darn!" Neona stamped her foot in a burst of orange light. "Don't tell me we blew it!"

"Hmm." Francie was thoughtful. "Magic like that just doesn't go to waste."

Fiona was pointing to a corner of the ledge. "Wh-wh-what's that?" she said, cowering away from the dark lump in the shadows.

It looked like a fallen animal. Darcy and Sam crept toward it cautiously. Sam poked it with his boot, but it didn't move.

"Here's the magic," he said, reaching down and picking up a huge pelt. "Fur coats! I'll bet there's one here for each of us."

Darcy picked one up and realized it was a whole bodysuit. "It's got legs and everything," she said stepping into it.

Fiona took one from Sam and cooed, "Ooh! Extra soft."

"I wonder what type of fur it is," Claw said, squirming a little.

"Don't worry," Hoshi answered. "It's synthetic."

"And check it out," Sam said, finding a stack of

framed objects under the pelt. "Snowshoes!"

"That'll keep us from sinking into the drifts!" Francie said. She spun around in her fur, then tickled Hoshi under the chin. "You guys are the best!"

"This is great," Sam said, strapping on his snowshoes. With this gear, we'll make it to Monsterville in no time."

"Let's go," Claw said, ducking outside. He reached in and pulled Fiona onto his shoulders. "Something tells me that it's now or never!"

The snow was still falling, but Darcy didn't mind anymore. She was toasty warm, and the snowshoes kept her on top of the snow.

We look like a pack of bears! she thought as they lumbered down the trail. The fairies rode inside their pelts, and Claw led the way, breaking the wind.

By the time they reached the crystal cave, Darcy's nerves were thrumming. She was so excited for Claw! He'd come so far, and now he was just steps away from home. But what if the cubs didn't recognize him? Would Monsterville welcome him, after so long?

At the entrance to the town of ghouls, the only sign of life was a few fairies napping on their giant mushrooms. The group stepped quietly around them and headed toward the woods where the yetis lived in snow huts.

Halfway down the trail, Darcy heard the squeaky laughter of yeti cubs.

"There!" She pointed to two cubs, tickling each other with daisies.

"It's Ay and Dee," Fiona said.

"My sons," Claw said under his breath. Gently he lowered Fiona to the ground. Then he strode ahead, marching toward the two yetis.

The cubs blinked up at him, pulling back in curiosity. A moment later, they scrambled ahead, climbing up his towering legs to his arms.

"Father!" Dee shrieked.

"What took you so long? We've been waiting," Ay babbled. "Eff has a new tooth. And Cee is grounded for chewing up the grass."

"Is that right?" Claw laughed, then hugged them closer. "I can see that I've missed a lot."

The yetis' shrieks brought their mother running, and soon the entire den of cubs was swarming around Claw. They hugged his legs. They climbed on his back. They ruffled the fur on his head.

"It's so good to see you," Marta told him.

Claw's huge arms enveloped her in a hug. "I've missed you. I was beginning to wonder if I'd make it."

"But we told him he'd get home," Fiona chimed in. "We promised. And we pulled him on the sled.

Francie dressed him up as a dog. And Darcy got him medicine. And I got to ride on his shoulders."

"You did all that?" Gee was fascinated.

"Cool!" Ay gushed.

"It's good to see Claw back at home," Francie said.

"Finally," Darcy agreed.

"I guess the legend of the Claw will die down for a while now," Sam said. "I'll have to come up with another fireside story to scare Fiona."

Floating above them, the three fairies twinkled.

"There's nothing as warm and fuzzy as a good deed," Hoshi said, sighing.

"That's for sure." Francie linked her arm through Darcy's and gave her friend a squeeze. "And now I know that good deeds can happen anywhere, any time."

"You *don't* have to be a fairy to help people," Darcy said.

"Nope." Francie's green eyes flashed. "You can always rely on girl power!"

There's more spooky

adventure coming your way in

New Grrrl in Town

by R. A. Noonan

Here's a spine-tingling preview . . .

Prologue

In the foothills of Montana's Bitterroot Mountains, spring had arrived. Crocuses had pushed up through the soft, muddy ground. Trees were putting forth tender new leaves.

Higher up, though, winter still ruled. Snow cloaked the mountains' rocky shoulders. Ice bound the streams. Low in the twilit sky, a nearly full moon glowed white.

Into the still air rose a wavering cry.

A hunting owl, hearing the sound, abruptly reversed course and flew the other way. A deer bolted in terror. In its den, a sleeping coyote awoke with a start, the hair on its back bristling.

The chilling cry swelled again. It came from a huge, shaggy, black creature crouched on a dome of rock. The beast looked like a wolf. But no wolf was ever this big. And no wolf's eyes ever looked like this—glowing golden, full of a fierce awareness that was neither animal nor human. Because the beast on the rock was neither one.

She was a werewolf.

As the last echoes died, the werewolf lowered her head. Her ears drooped. There had been no answering howl. So it was just as they'd told her— she was alone. There were no others of her kind roaming these mountains anymore.

I'm the only one, she thought. *The only one who's not old and fat and toothless. The others—hah! They might as well be lap-dogs!*

Her lip curled back from her fangs, and a low growl rippled from her throat. The thought of the others infuriated her. What kind of self-respecting werewolf stayed in on a perfect night like tonight, when the air was alive with the scent of prey?

She could just picture them. Right about now, they were probably chowing down on defrosted steaks and whimpering at reruns of *Lassie*. Grrr!

"Kowabunga!"

Even in the still mountain air, the yell was so faint and faraway that no ordinary ears would have caught it. But werewolf ears are not ordinary. At the sound, the giant beast's head swiveled sharply. She sprang to her feet, and her keen eyes scanned the twilit slopes far below her.

Aha. There they were—two humans on mountain bikes. Boys. Teenagers. They were racing down a trail at top speed, toward the lights of the nearby town. Late for dinner, the werewolf guessed. It was about that time, wasn't it? . . . Her belly rumbled.

As she stared at the distant figures, her golden eyes narrowed. *What I need is some fresh blood. Young blood. Mmm. What if . . . yes, why not?*

Licking her lips, the great wolf jumped from the rock and began trotting easily toward the town lights.

"Fiona!" Sam Mackie yelled through the open window. "If you make me late again, I'm going to be really mad. Let's go! Get a move on!"

"Sam," his mother's exasperated voice came from the kitchen. "Stop yelling. You've got forty-five minutes until school starts. How many times have I told you to be more patient with your sister? She's only six, for heaven's sake."

"Yeah, yeah." Sam thumped his backpack down on the porch floor and leaned against the railing. Moodily he pushed his dark, curly hair off his forehead.

He wasn't worried about being late for school. But he was sick of getting there at the last minute every morning, and never having any time to hang out with the guys. His family had moved to Whiterock, Montana, months ago, but he still felt like a stranger a lot of the time. How was he supposed to get to know anyone, if all his free time was spent shepherding his little sister around?

"Hey, Mackie!"

Two of Sam's seventh-grade classmates were standing in the street. One of them was Arnie Andersen, co-captain of the baseball team and its star pitcher. The other was Mark Williams, their power hitter. Sam had barely made the team—he was only a relief catcher. He'd never had much chance to play ball back in Chicago, although he was a die-hard Cubs fan.

"Let's go, man," Arnie called. He held up a hand-held video game player. "I just got Kung Fu Masters IV. You've got to check it out."

Sam's heart sank. He'd been dying to try the new game. Also, he really would have liked the chance to hang with Arnie and Mark. They were cool.

But he couldn't leave Fiona. His parents would kill him. "I'll be along in a few minutes," he called. "I have to walk my little sister to the bus."

Mark shook his head. "I don't know, Mackie," he said in a disgusted voice. "You're always hanging around with girls—*little* girls. I'm starting to wonder about you. Why don't you ditch her?"

"Maybe I will—tomorrow," Sam said lamely. His ears were bright red.

Arnie laughed. "Whatever. We'll catch you later, maybe."

They sauntered away down the street. Sam kicked the porch rail angrily. It was so unfair! Couldn't his mom and dad see that Fiona was ruining his life? Scowling, he kicked the rail again.

At that moment Fiona walked out the front door. "Why are you kicking the porch, Sammy?" she wanted to know. "Poor porch, I bet you hurt its feelings."

Sam rolled his eyes and went down the steps. "Porches don't have feelings."

"How do you know?" Fiona asked. "Poor porchie. Poorchie porchie." She tossed her dark curls happily as she followed her brother. "Poorchie, porchie, lorchie, storchie!" she sang.

"Just shut up, all right?" Sam growled. "Or if you have to sing, sing something that isn't stupid."

Fiona fell silent with a hurt look on her face.

"Oh, brother," Sam muttered. "What next?"

Fiona went to Whiterock Elementary, on the other side of town from the Mackies' house. Every morning, she and several other kids caught the school bus near the middle school, where Sam went.

He and Fiona walked in silence until they were only a block away. Then they both turned at the sound of someone calling their names.

It was Darcy Ryan, their cousin. She pedaled toward them on her bicycle, her blond braids flopping over her shoulders. "Hey, you guys," she called with a grin.

"Hi!" Fiona ran to meet her.

"Hey." Sam's greeting was less enthusiastic. Ordinarily, he was glad to see his cousin. She was a good friend, even though she was only a fifth grader. She'd really helped him through those first rough weeks of living in Whiterock. But right now, all he could think was: *Another girl. How did I get stuck with all these girls?*

"Know what? I think I heard a wolf howling in the mountains last night," Darcy said. She jumped off her bike and walked it along the sidewalk next to her cousins. "There used to be tons of wolves around here, but hunters drove most of them away years ago. It would be so cool if they came back, don't you think?"

"Big whoop," Sam said.

"What's wrong with him?" Darcy asked Fiona, throwing Sam a surprised look.

"I don't know. He's being really mean today. Maybe he hurt his toe when he kicked the porch," Fiona suggested.

"Huh? Kicked the porch?" Darcy repeated.

Sam hunched his shoulders and strode on ahead. He didn't want to hear Fiona describing how he had kicked the porch, and he hated it when people talked about him as if he wasn't there.

Besides, he could see Arnie and Mark and a couple of other guys ahead, and he'd rather they didn't see him walking with Fiona and Darcy. Not after what Mark had said that morning.

He was staring at the ground as he walked, and he didn't notice the white shape creeping toward him over a broad, fenced-in lawn. But then a menacing growl sounded, just a few feet away. Slowly Sam turned his head, knowing—dreading—what he was going to see. Oh no, he thought.

Sam was no chicken. He'd had his share of wild times since he'd moved to Whiterock. In fact, some of the adventures he'd had were beyond most people's wildest dreams. And he'd faced plenty of scares without flinching. But he did have one secret fear. A fear that was as deep as it was embarrassing.

Sam Mackie was terrified of dogs.

It had started way back when he was four. The neighbor's Alsatian had gone crazy one day while Sam was playing in the front yard of their Chicago house. When Sam's mother came out, she'd found the little boy cowering under the stoop while the dog barked and tried to get at him.

Ever since that day, Sam had kept his distance from dogs. He'd learned to tolerate the smaller ones, the ones with long floppy ears and soulful eyes. But the sight of a big, mean dog was always guaranteed to start his heart thudding.

As it was now. Because Sam was face-to-face with Baxter, the biggest, meanest dog in Whiterock. And there was only a thin, wire cyclone fence between them.

Baxter belonged to Dr. Bernstein, the principal of Sam's school. Dr. Bernstein had had him no more than a couple of weeks. None of the kids at school knew where the principal had gotten Baxter, but Sam had heard rumors that the dog was part wolf. He certainly looked fierce enough. He had cold, pale eyes like chips of blue glass. He had massive shoulders and gleaming fangs. And his coat was pure, snowy white.

Baxter stared at Sam through the diamond-pattern mesh of the fence. Sam stared back, feeling like a bird facing a snake.

Baxter's top lip rippled back from his teeth. The growl sounded again. Then suddenly he burst into a fit of barking.

Sam jumped backward without thinking, tripped over his own feet, and crashed to the ground.

"No! Don't move, Sam!" he heard Darcy yell.

Sam froze, still sitting on the ground. But it was too late.

Baxter went crazy. His barking got more and more frenzied. Foam flecks started flying from his mouth. He dashed from side to side as if looking for a way through the fence. Then he gathered his powerful hind legs under him and sprang.

Baxter was coming over the fence!